Cheers.
VERonique 2012

The Pink Hat

Veronique Perrier Mandal

THE PINK HAT

First Edition
Copyright © 2012   Veronique Perrier Mandal

Published by Middlebranch Publishing
Middlebranchpublishing@ymail.com

ISBN-13: 978-0-9880132-0-9
ISBN-10: 978-0-9880132-0-9

Cover designed by
Jason Kryk and Veronique Perrier Mandal

ACKNOWLEDGEMENTS

Nothing happens in our lives in isolation. Therefore, in the writing of this book I have to thank the following people who have contributed in numerous ways including being first readers, proof readers and copy editors. Because they wanted me to be successful they did not offer gratuitous praise and for that I am truly grateful. Because of their collective integrity they made many helpful observations which I included in the final draft of The Pink Hat. Here they are - each one should be listed first but alas, we are limited by the dimension of words on paper.

My fabulous sisters Beth, Marilyn, Pauline and Leona who are super critics. I certainly breathed a sigh of relief when they signed off on the story. Catherine White, whose insightful comments helped shaped the beginning of the book. Anne Winterbottom, for her fine copy editing. Jeff Boulton, the first guy to read Pink Hat made wonderful suggestions that had me writing more into the story. Photojournalist Jason Kryk for his beautiful cover. Amanda Gellman, Faye Johnson, Carol Derbyshire, Elizabeth Davis, Jeanie Laforge, Tim Jamieson, the second guy to read it, and Fran Funaro. Thank you also to my colleagues Larry Forsyth and Martin Vaughan. A very special thank you to Chris Edwards, publisher of Walkerville Publishing, for his invaluable help in the final production of The Pink Hat.

My dear friend Suzi Marsh Hattie who read the first half-finished draft and liked it enough to constantly be on my case to get it finished. My friend and fellow thespian Felicity Bryant in Wales and Paula Bond whose encouragement never falters.

Thank you all.

No greater thanks could go to my sons Rajesh and Bijan and husband Christopher Vander Doelen. They always make me believe there is nothing I can't do and they always have my back. Thank you Christopher for your masterful editing and loving me the way you do.

For
Marguerite and Richard
Barbara and Nick
Iris and Ron

LOMPOC, California

When I was eight years old I spied on my father. My discovery haunted my childhood and had an unimaginable impact on the rest of my life.

One Saturday afternoon after I heard him pull down the ladder to the attic I crept up, stuck my head through the hole and saw him take a dark pink, wide brimmed hat out of an old trunk. He caressed it, stared out the window and rubbed his hand across his eyes. It seemed to me that he was crying. I wanted to rush over to him and ask about the hat but something told me I shouldn't.

Quietly slipping down the ladder I went into the kitchen where my mom was making rhubarb pie. My dad's favourite. I watched mom wipe her hands on her yellow apron, an Easter gift from Dad. She told me the colour always makes her feel happy which is why she wears it all the time. She was humming one of her favourite songs and seeing me come in to the room, smiled and held up a big stalk of rhubarb. I took it and started munching. She continued to hum and began making a fluted edge on the pie. This was not a woman worried about a pink hat in a trunk.

There was a mystery in our house and from then on I kept waiting for Dad to say something about the pink hat. He never did. The following summer I announced I needed a new sun hat and asked Mom if we could go to Macy's to buy me a big brimmed pink hat I saw in the window. She said it was a good idea and we had great fun buying my new hat. During our shopping trip I tried to get her to reveal anything she might know about the hat in the trunk.

"Do you really like this one? I think it could be a darker pink."

"That pink looks beautiful on you dear. Why would you want something darker?" she asked, giving me her "Is there something more to this?" kind of look.

"Oh, I was just wondering. Have you ever seen a hat that's a darker pink?"

"Since I've never really wanted a pink hat, I've never really noticed. Well, shall we take this one?" Then, that look again.

"OK. Thanks Mom."

I couldn't wait to get home to show Dad and see his reaction. He smiled and said I looked great in pink.

"You're a stunner, Angel. Pink is definitely your colour."

Not quite the reaction I was hoping for and I had to ask, "Would a darker pink be better for me?"

He never flinched. "I don't think so. That hat is perfect for you."

Occasionally, when they were both out of the house I would pull down the ladder and go up to take a look at the trunk that guarded the Pink Secret, as I came to think of it. It was always locked and no matter how hard I searched the key was never to be found.

I began having fantasies about the person who owned that hat. I knew it definitely wasn't mom's because on the hat shopping trip she told me she always preferred plain white hats.

During the last weekend in August, the year I was starting senior high, I learned a little more. At least I was convinced it had something to do with the Pink Secret. I was looking for Dad to ask if we could go to the beach. Mom said he probably wouldn't because the first Saturday in September was the day dad gave our dusty old attic its annual clean. I hadn't noticed but once she pointed it out to me, I remembered that the day I saw Dad in the attic was a Saturday in September. Then I began to remember other summers when we had to make sure we were home from holiday before the first Saturday in September. And no one ever explained why.

It was all so intriguing and I wanted so badly to know what Mom knew or if she suspected Dad had a pink secret. I looked for signs there was trouble between them, but they always seemed happy and in love. That made the Pink Secret even more tantalizing. Some day, I used to tell myself, some day I will learn about the memories hidden in that darn trunk.

High school became the focus of my life. School work, learning to drive, best friends and boys often kept me from the attic for months on end. At least until September rolled around and I waited to see if Dad made his annual pilgrimage. He always did. Every year I asked if I could help him and he always refused.

The only chink in his emotional control of the Pink Secret came the summer I was leaving for college. I was moving to New York to study Visual Arts at Columbia University and Mom suggested I buy a steamer trunk and have some of my stuff sent my train. Turning to Dad I asked if we had any old trunks in the attic. He turned a dangerous shade of white and I thought he was going to faint. My mother, oblivious to Dad's scary pallor, said she seemed to remember a couple of old trunks going up there when they moved in.

By the time he spoke Dad had recovered and jokingly said "That old trunk has a terrible moth ball smell that would ruin all those expensive clothes you buy Angel. I'd be much happier to spend money on a new trunk than more new clothes."

We bought a new trunk.

About a month after I started school I got a part-time job at Macy's and came home for only two days at Christmas. I arrived Christmas Eve and left Boxing Day morning. I worked full time in the summer so Mom and Dad came to visit me. In October I met Paul, a senior from San Diego. My new, hot love banished the Pink Secret. School work and sex occupied the next two years. Paul graduated and moved to Texas and whenever I had time off I headed to the Lone Star State or he came to New York.

It was a heady time in my life. I was doing well at school and soon left my retail job for a paid internship at the Guggenheim Museum. It was a triumph to beat out almost forty other students for the coveted internship. I went home for two weeks the Christmas before I graduated. Paul and his parents came to celebrate the season and our engagement. Except for fleeting moments I had not given much thought to the Pink Secret for almost four years.

Two months after graduation Mom died following a series of heart attacks. I spent the last three days of her life in her hospital room, saying all the mother-daughter things we wouldn't get to talk about.

"Angel, I'm so sorry I won't be able to shop for a wedding dress with you. It's something every mother of a daughter dreams about. I planned to give you my grandmother's pearls on your wedding day, but I want to give them to you now. There's a velvet covered box in my suitcase in the closet, could you bring it to me."

I find the box beneath the clothes Mom had worn to the hospital. Everything seems surreal and I'm going through the motions of normalcy like a sleepwalker. I sit back on her bed and place the box on the sheet covering her frail body. She slowly lifts the lid.

"Give me your hand." With all the strength she can summon, Mom lifts the beautiful double strand of pearls from the box and places them in my outstretched hand. She rests her fingers on them and caresses my wrist. I bite the inside of my lower lip to stop from crying.

"Have your dad put these on for you on your wedding day and know that I will be there, so proud of you. Will you still get married here in Lompoc?"

"Oh Mom, of course. This is my home and it's where you and Dad made a wonderful life for me. I wouldn't consider getting married anywhere else."

"I'm glad. Your father will like that. Have you been making your guest list?"

"Yes. We're up to about 140 so far and we haven't included Paul's old school buddies and some of my friends from New York. Paul says we shouldn't go over 200 because we'll never get to talk to everyone. Even 200 is daunting."

"Would you mind inviting my friends from the bridge club? They've all been hinting they want to be there and I half agreed, but I said I had to check with you and Paul. It will mean a lot to them. Just in case, they've all written out their names and addresses for invitations and I've left it on my desk in the house. Most of them you know. Emma Simms joined us last year after Sissy died. She hinted that since she was taking over from Sissy she should also be on your invitation list."

We laugh and I assure her they will all be included. "I'm having three showers. I know that seems crazy but the girls in New York want me to come there for a weekend for one, my friends in Dallas are having one and Paul's friends are organizing another couples event. I'll be worn out before the wedding day."

"But you'll love every minute of it. Oh God I feel cheated. I just need a few more months. I'm sorry Angel. Tell me, do you and Paul plan to have children?"

I nod.

"I would love to have been a grandmother. I tried not to spoil you but I would have loved spoiling my grandchildren. Treat my grandchildren well. Tell them I would have been a great grandma."

Every time tears threatened, Mom would tell me she wanted to talk, not grieve.

"I feel very sorry for myself right now Angel, but I don't want to waste these precious moments with you grieving. I am trying to be grateful to have these extra days that many parents are denied. Would you read to me? Read The Road Not Taken.

I reached over and picked up one of her favourite books of poetry from the bedside table, lay down beside her and began to read...

Two roads diverged in a yellow wood
And sorry I could not travel both
And be one traveler, long I stood
And looked down one as far as I could
To where it bent in the undergrowth

Then took the other, as just as fair
And having perhaps the better claim
Because it was grassy and wanted wear;
Though as for that the passing there
Had worn them really about the same,
And both that morning equally lay
In leaves no step had trodden black.
Oh, I marked the first for another day!
Yet knowing how way leads on to way,
I doubted if I should ever come back.
I shall be telling this with a sigh
Somewhere ages and ages hence:
Two roads diverged in a wood, and I,
I took the one less traveled by,
And that has made all the difference.

I put down the book and begin to recite one of my favourite childhood poems, one by Joyce Kilmer that Mom taught me when I was in third grade.

I think that I shall never see
A poem lovely as a tree

A tree whose hungry mouth is prest
Against the earth's sweet flowing breast;

A tree that looks at God all day,
And lifts her leafy arms to pray;

A tree that may in Summer wear
A nest of robins in her hair;

Upon whose bosom snow has lain;
Who intimately lives with rain.

Poems are made by fools like me,
But only God can make a tree.

As I finished the poem I felt her hand slip from my arm and my heart lurched. I soon realized she had fallen asleep so I quietly slid off the bed and went outside where Dad was waiting.

"Are you okay Angel? Why don't you go down to the cafeteria. Paul is there. I'll sit with Mom."

"I was reading some Robert Frost."

"One of her favourites. I'll read some more, just in case she can hear me. She always loved to have us read to her." His eyes fill with tears and he can't continue. He briefly hugged me and went into mom's room.

The following day mom seemed brighter. Dad, Paul and I ate our meals with her and she gave Paul the speech about the importance of being friends and never letting the sun set on an argument. There was a lot of laughter despite the pain we were all feeling. Around 5 p.m. Paul left to go to the airport to pick up mom's sister Carrie Ann. Dad left to get a newspaper.

"I'll let you and Angel have some mother daughter time."

He kissed mom gently on the lips, holding her small face between his hands. His pain made me want to scream. Mom smiled, looking at him as though she could see into his very soul. "Hurry back darling."

I crawled up on the bed with her, carefully avoiding the tubes that stretched across the blankets. I was tortured by the guilt of wanting to ask her about the pink hat.

"Angel, there's something on your mind. Why don't you get it off your chest."

That was Mom. She never missed anything when it came to reading my face. I didn't think I was even conscious of the question flitting across my mind all afternoon. Taking a deep breath I casually asked her if she had ever seen the inside of Dad's old trunk in the attic. She smiled knowingly.

"Yes, I have. And yes, I know about the pink hat. But your father doesn't know that I know. He forgot that when we first met and were still strangers he told me about the hat and the woman who owns it."

"Who is she?"

"I'll let your father tell you that story." She reached for my hand. "Never forget for a moment that I know your father has loved me and would never do anything to hurt me. He has been a wonderful husband and friend and a great father, but I've always known there was a small piece of his heart that belonged to that pink hat. And how do you know about it? What do you know?"

"I sneaked a look in the attic one day when I was eight and saw him looking at it."

"Did you ask him about it?"

"No. I couldn't."

"I'm glad." She tires and we are quiet. I have tried so hard but my grief explodes inside my heart.

"Oh Mom."

"I know dear. I hate this too. But there is nothing we can do about it." She looked so frail and tired but still beautiful. I tucked her short, brown hair behind her ears and tied the blue ribbons holding her bed jacket together.

"I'll miss you. I love you so much."

"I know Angel and I love you so very much. I'm sorry to cause you this pain. But you know I'm not going far."

I lay as close to her as I can get, holding her hand and we slept. Dad woke me at 2 a.m. and mom slept on. We buried her three days later. Those days were filled with unbearable grief, cherished friendships and laughter. I will never get over losing my mother.

I stayed with Dad for two weeks, helping to deal with mom's belongings, giving some away and keeping her treasures, especially those she left to each of us. Dad didn't talk much for the first week. His sense of loss was profound. They had been married more than twenty years.

Although he could have retired several years earlier he had decided to continue part-time work with the military and is now glad for that distraction.

My internship at the Guggenheim turned into a full time job and I loved it. Paul and I spent many weekends flying between Dallas and New York. The long distance romance bothered him more than it did me. The Christmas after Mom died he asked me to set a date to get married. I reluctantly resigned from the Guggenheim in April and Dad walked me down the aisle the end of June. I chose the Saturday prior to the anniversary of mom's death because, somehow, despite not having her with us, it made her feel closer. After a honeymoon in Europe, Paul and I settled in Dallas where many of Paul's major clients were based. I would have preferred to stay in New York.

We kept in close touch with Dad and had him spend holidays with us whenever he could. He and Paul got along well and genuinely enjoyed each other's company. He was lonely but the arrival of our son David two years after we were married seemed to give him a new lease on life.

On our fourteenth anniversary Paul and I had a fierce row over something that started out small and escalated with me announcing I "wanted out." It was probably a storm that had been brewing for several years, maybe even since before getting married when I had to give up my job at the Guggenheim. I never found a job in Dallas that could match the excitement of the museum and after David was born decided to take a couple of years off. When he was five and in kindergarten, I started a part-time job at the Easel Art Shop. I would have preferred to work at the Dallas Museum of Art but the only job openings I was interested in were full time and I knew they would require too much time away from David and Paul in the evenings. We began sleeping in separate rooms but maintained a civil relationship while we seemed to tacitly decide to "see what happens." I didn't tell Dad.

About three months into our separation, life sent me yet another challenge. Struggling into the kitchen with an armload of groceries at lunch time on a Tuesday I hear the phone ringing but can't get to it in time. The message machine kicks in and I hear Dad's doctor leaving a message to call him immediately. I grab the phone before he rings off and learn Dad had suffered a heart attack the previous evening and been admitted to the Lompoc Valley

Medical Center. He suggests I might want to come to Lompoc immediately since they were not yet sure how seriously his heart has been damaged. I call Paul and within a few hours we've dropped David off at Paul's mother's house and were on a plane to Lompoc.

It's a shock to see my strong, robust, healthy father ensnared in tubes and electronic wires that beep out signals he is still alive. I begin to cry. Not again I think. Dad opens his eyes and holds out his arms.

"Come here Angel. It's not as bad as it looks." I hug him, carefully so as not to dislodge any of the life-giving tubing.

While answering the questions I needed to ask I sense he has something on his mind besides the heart attack. I soon discover what it is and his next words were to send me on a journey that had started the day I spied on him in the attic.

"Take my wallet from the drawer. Now, take out the small key in the inside pouch."

"What's this?"

"I want you to take this key, go up into the attic and open an old trunk that sits under the window."

I am visibly stunned.

"In the trunk you'll find a dark pink hat and a big brown envelope. I want you to bring them to me. No. Don't ask now. Please just go get them."

Shocked, I just nod. Paul takes my arm and we leave.

"What's this about?"

"I am not sure but we are soon going to get answers to something that's been bugging me for over twenty years."

In the attic my hands shake as I hold a key that is about to unlock a family secret. "I'm not sure I want to do this."

"Why not?"

"Maybe I don't want to know what this is all about."

"Yes, you do. And your father asked you to do it."

The lock clicks open and I slowly lift the heavy lid. There it is, sitting in all its dark pink splendour. I lift it out of the trunk. Paul reaches in and picks up the brown envelope, lowers the lid and turns the key in the lock. I am so mesmerized I have no idea if there is anything else in the trunk.

Downstairs, I stop in front of the mirror in the hallway. I can't resist. I lift the hat and pull it down on my long blond hair. It is gorgeous. I stand there, transfixed.

"That looks beautiful on you. But come on Angel. Your father is waiting for this."

I say very little in the car. My mind is filled with questions and I clutch the hat in my lap.

When I place the hat close to my dad's hand, he caresses it in the same way I saw him do it when I was eight. Paul hands him the envelope which Dad asks him to open. Reaching inside he draws out one wrinkled air mail letter, opens it and hands it to Dad who slowly reads a few lines and hands it to me.

"Find her. Please Angel. I want to see her once more before I die. I want to know she's ok and happy."

"Don't say that. You're not going to die. Who is she and where would we find her?"

"Her name is Angelique LaPierre. She's a Canadian I met when I was stationed in Bermuda. I fell in love with her when she was nineteen and I was twenty-seven. I wanted her to marry me but she went off to see the world. She kept in touch for a while then my letters started getting returned. I went to England once to find her. I saw her name on a theatre billboard and went in to see the show. I tried to see her after the show but I was told she left as soon as the curtain came down because it was closing night and she was leaving town the next day. In the morning I went to the last address I had for her but the woman who answered the door said she didn't know where she was living. I left without talking to her.

"I came back and continued to fly with her hat in the cockpit of my plane for another seven years, until I met your mother just after I was stationed in Vandenberg. We got married and I put the hat in the trunk. After your mother died I thought of looking for her again but didn't know where to start. That's the last letter I received. There are many others in this envelope and others in the bottom of the trunk. Perhaps you'll find a clue in them that I missed. I know this is a needle in a haystack, but please do this for me."

"You want to tell us the whole story?"

"Not right now."

A nurse arrived and said Dad should get some sleep. We leave, reluctantly.
"So?"

"So what do you think of your father's request, this whole situation?"

"I don't know what to think. It's bizarre to hang on to a hat of an old girlfriend."

"Guess she wasn't just any old girlfriend. Must have really been something. What do you want to do? My new partner is working out really well so I can take time away from the office and since you don't like your job you could take a leave of absence."

"Let's go back to the attic."

Taking another stack of letters from the trunk, we spread them out with those in the brown envelope and begin reading, trying to piece together a sketchy route of where she had gone in the first few years after leaving Bermuda.

In the twentieth letter Paul finds a few more clues.

"She became a nurse - that's a jump from acting. Look, here's the name of the hospital. We have the name of the theatre and the hospital and friends' names she's mentioned from time to time in the other letters."

"Guess we're going to England. Wait, what if she's living in Canada now? Dad said she's Canadian."

"We have a lot more to go on in England than we do here. Let's take the letters with us and make a list of everyone and every place she mentions."

"You don't really have to do this Paul."

"I want to. We're not divorced yet and I have to say I am pretty curious about all this. By the way, did you notice anything familiar about her name?"

"Angelique."

"Angelique. Angeline. Just a coincidence? I wonder if your mother knew her name."

"I'm sure she did. I don't want to go there right now. Here's a letter that mentions names of friends in Bermuda. They were Americans. Perhaps we can track them down first. It seems from the way she writes about them that Dad also knew the two women. Darn, she only uses their first names."

"Perhaps your dad can remember. We'll ask him tomorrow."

Dad was in good spirits and remembered the women very well.

"I seem to remember that Jessie Wells, the older of the two, was from New Jersey but she died on her way to England to marry an English naval officer she met in Bermuda and I know that Bridget O'Neill was from South Braintree, Massachusetts. She wrote to me for many years but I never kept her letters."

"But Dad, that's where she lived more than forty years ago. Talk about a needle in a haystack."

"I know Angel. Just do the best you can. If they can patch up my heart the way they say they can you might have a bit longer to search."

"Did Bridget ever tell you she got married or anything else that Angeline and I could go on?"

"I believe she did get married but she was still living in South Braintree. It's hard to remember after so many years."

"Well, you focus on your health and Paul and I will see what we can do. Paul would you mind getting the car?"

"Take it easy Mark. We'll do our best."

"Thanks Paul. I'm grateful."

"I'll meet you downstairs Angeline."

"Angel? Is everything OK with you and Paul? I just sense something is not, well, I just sense something."

"Don't start worrying about us. We're working on it. Nothing most couples don't go through. Don't stress about it. I need you to get better. We're going to find Angelique. Speaking of which - about my name?"

"Your mother chose it. I was somewhat surprised but she insisted. She never did tell me why. Just said she loved the sound of it. Now give me one of those wonderful hugs and let me get some sleep."

Leaving the hospital, my mind cannot fathom my mother giving me a name so close to that of the woman who still obviously held a piece of Dad's heart. Perhaps she loved him that much. It made me appreciate her even more, knowing she had such a unique depth of understanding of how Dad felt about Angelique. Yet, she never let on to him that she even knew about the woman. I missed mom so much in that moment the pain brought tears.

Paul looked at me with a raised eyebrow but remained silent when I shook my head. He knew enough not to ask.

"Let's fly to Boston next Thursday. That will give us another few days to make sure your dad is making progress. South Braintree is only ten or eleven miles from Logan airport. We'll start by looking up all the O'Neill's in the phone book and if necessary check out the high schools and their yearbooks."

"Sounds great. Thank you."

"Are you sure you're OK with all of this? It must seem awfully strange."

"It is on one level, but I've wondered about that pink hat and its owner for so long I just want to get the whole story and I won't do that unless we find Angelique. Sure hope it won't freak her out if we do find her. Let's eat. I'm starved. Are you sure Janice won't mind having David stay at her house?"

"When my sister says 'the more the merrier' she actually means it."

"And with four teenagers of her own. She's a wonder. You know, David could stay home on his own. But I'd prefer he stay with Janice. "

"I hope David won't mind too much. He doesn't mind hanging out with his cousins for a few hours but finds the noise and chaos hard to take for long periods."

"Oh well, it will certainly make him appreciate how good he has it at home as an only child. He does love Janice's cooking, or more specifically all the baking she does for her brood. He keeps asking why I don't make my own bread like she does, and why I buy doughnuts from the bakery when Aunt Janice whips them up in no time at all. You know, one could dislike your sister."

"Yeah, but she does send us over samples of her labours. It's her thing. She's a committed homemaker. Not that you aren't Angel, but it's all Janice has ever wanted - to have a brood and spend every waking hour looking after them. That's one reason Eric insists on a once a week date. It's the one night when he can have her all to himself."
Later, lying alone in the big bed she once shared with Paul, Angeline found herself wondering what would become of them and how she would react if she did meet Angelique. She had a feeling her father's request

would bring many changes into their lives and hopes she is doing the right thing. Figuring only time will tell, she fell into a restless sleep.

BOSTON, Massachusetts

April is lovely in Boston. Renting a car at the airport we drive to South Braintree and check into a quaint New England bed and breakfast. Choosing to be economical meant we would be sharing a room for the first time in many months, albeit in twin beds.

Paul immediately got out the phonebook and scanned the Os

"The good news is there are O'Neills in South Braintree. The bad news is there are almost thirty of them. Let's get calling."

"Wait. What are we going to say?"

"We'll say we are looking for Bridget O'Neill because we have a message from a friend she knew in Bermuda. Not exactly accurate but it'll do."

Paul made the first five calls, I made the next five. Seven said they didn't know a Bridget O'Neill and three were answering machines suggesting the caller leave a message. We did. Ten more calls without success and we needed a break. After a quick shower and change of clothes we went out to find a place to eat. Dinner at the New Englander was pleasant and provided excellent home cooked fare. The chef even came out to see if we were enjoying the meal.

Identifying us as visitors he asks what brought us to Braintree. We give him the Coles Notes version that includes only the fact we are trying to track down a friend called Bridget O'Neill.

"Jack O'Neill had a daughter Bridget. She was the oldest of his five kids. He died last year. I think one of his sons works at the Braintree Blues Bar on Main Street. It's a ten minute walk from here. He might be able to help you."

We thanked him and hit the BBB which reminded us of a favourite bar on Bourbon Street in New Orleans. We found seats at the bar and ordered rum and coke. Ted, the talkative bartender, told us he was 42 and had just gotten married. He'd also become an instant parent to three teenagers - a boy and two girls. When he took a breath we asked if he knew a Bridget O'Neill who had lived in Bermuda when she was a teenager.

"That's weird. My sister is Bridget O'Neill and she lived in Bermuda when she was eighteen. She was there three years. Why do you want to know?"

"We're trying to find one of her roommates - a Canadian - and we hoped Bridget might know where we could find her."

"That would be Angelique. Bridget talked about her all the time. She was really sick most of the time she lived in Bermuda. I think Bridget said she left to go to England. Bridget came home a year later."

"Does she still live around here?"

"Not in Braintree. They moved to Boston about ten years ago. But they're away in Vegas."
"When do you expect them back?"

"Day after tomorrow."

"Would you mind giving me Bridget's contact information so that we can get in touch with her when they return?"

"I guess that would be ok. You're not axe murderers are you?" he asks jokingly.

Paul and I instinctively pull out ID to show the guy.

"We just want to ask about Angelique. But please feel free to alert her that we'll be contacting her."

"Hey, no problem. Here's her phone numbers and her address. "

Arriving in Boston the next morning we checked in at the historic Omni Parker House hotel. We both love the city and decide to spend the day being tourists. But first, we drive to Bridget's address to check it out so as not to waste time once she agrees to see us. We hope.

We find Bridget's house in the City Point neighbourhood of South Boston.

After some discussion Paul and I vote to wait until Monday to make the call, giving her time to get home, unpack and take a breath before being confronted by a couple of strangers.

Sharing a room but sleeping in separate beds is unnerving. After a day of sightseeing, dinner in a small bistro and dancing in a popular night club some of the old spark between us threatens to ignite. As much as I want to, I explain to Paul this isn't the time. We are on an adventure that seems to be stripping away at layers of problems we have not resolved. Maybe that will ultimately prove to be a good thing. I don't know. But I don't want to resume a sexual relationship without having figured out all the emotional baggage. To my surprise, Paul doesn't argue.

As much as I am looking forward to Monday morning, I dread it. I am partly afraid Bridget will not be able to tell us anything and partly afraid she will. Sleep Sunday night is elusive. In the morning my hands begin to sweat as I dial her number.

"Hello." I hear a cheerful voice with a soft, pronounced Bostonian accent.

"Hello." She says again.

"Oh, hello. Is this Bridget O'Neill?"

"Yes, O'Neill is my maiden name. Who's speaking?"

"My name is Angeline Forrester. My father is Mark Forrester. I believe you met him when you lived in Bermuda."

"Mark Forrester's daughter? I can't believe it. Yes, I knew Mark from Bermuda. Is something wrong?"

"Well, I'd like to talk to you in person if it's convenient. Would you have time to see me?"

"Of course. Where are you?"

"My husband and I are here in Boston. We're staying at the Omni Parker."

"Why don't you come out to my place for lunch? My goodness, Mark's daughter."

She gives me directions and I don't tell her we had already driven past her house.

"Well?"

"We're going to her place for lunch. 12:30."

"Let's go for coffee and pick up some flowers before we head out there."

Driving up Bridget's street my heart begins to pound in my chest and my hands sweat. Paul reaches over squeezing my clenched fist.
"This is what we've been waiting for. Try to relax. You said she sounds like a nice person."

"Yes. I know. I'll be fine."

We walk up the steps to the elegant brownstone on East Broadway. It's at the corner of a row and the yard is filled with shrubs surrounding colourful flower beds and a manicured lawn. A large honey locust tree shades the large front bay window and white concrete flower pots sit on three of the steps. The doorbell is on the right side of two ornately carved double wooden doors, each with leaded stain glass windows. I take a deep breath and push hard enough to hear it chime. The door is almost immediately opened by a small, pretty woman who looks younger than I figure her age to be, which is somewhere in her early sixties. Her short, nicely styled brown hair is filled with grey and her brown eyes seem to be laughing, as though they can't help themselves.

She welcomes us like long lost friends, her freckled round face breaking into a beaming smile.

"Come in. Come in. I'm Bridget O'Neill, St. James now."

"I'm Angeline and this is my husband Paul. Thank you so much for taking the time to see us."

"I'm delighted you called."

She ushers us into a cozy living room filled with early American furniture, books and family photos. Two floor to ceiling windows flank a stone fireplace. It looks lived in and loved.

"I have to say I am very intrigued by your visit. But I'll wait until I've offered you something to drink. Would you like tea? You probably want to talk before we have lunch. I'll put these lovely carnations in water. Thank you."

She soon returns with a tea tray that contains an old fashioned teapot, china cups and saucers, milk and sugar, napkins and a glass plate of homemade chocolate chip cookies.

True to her word she waits until we are all sipping tea before asking a question.

"First of all, how is your father?"

"He's had a serious heart attack but so far he is holding his own. He asked us to find Angelique. He wants to see her before...in case..."

"I'm sorry to hear about his heart attack but I can understand his request. He was so in love with Angelique and had his heart badly broken when she left."

"So she didn't love Dad?"

"Not in the way he wanted. Maybe if she had stayed, or if she were older, something might have changed, but to her he was one of the best friends she ever had. They got along so well and had many things in common, especially dancing. She loved to dance and so did your father. She called him her dancing flyboy. But she was on a career mission and it didn't include staying in Bermuda or settling down. I don't really think she understood how devastated he was when she told him she was leaving."

"How did they meet?"

"Well, I'm somewhat responsible for that."

"How so?"

"Well it all started about a month after Angelique arrived in Bermuda from Canada to work in a musical revue show directed by some guy who was also from Canada. One evening our other roommate Jessie asked us about our hobbies..."

BERMUDA

"What do you do when you're not acting Angie?

"I love to read, dance, horseback ride and I especially love hanging around airports watching planes come and go. I used to sit in the airport in Montreal for hours, sometimes all day on Saturday or Sunday. You sure meet interesting people in airports. You just have to be careful not to talk to the weirdos though, they can be scary. "

"It sounds like you keep pretty busy. Bridget isn't there an air show and open house on Kindley air base this weekend?"
"Next weekend."

"You should take Angie. They give tours of the base and you actually get to sit in some of the fighter planes."

"Would you like to go? I can get us tickets."

"I'd love to but I'm working Saturday so we would have to go on Sunday."

"That works for me. I've been out there dozens of times but it's always fun. There's a girl in our office who was asking if any of us wanted to go so I'll ask her for tickets. Want to meet at the Islander after your show tonight?"

"My favourite spot."

BERMUDA, KINDLEY AIR BASE
St. George's Island

"This is so fabulous. Thank you for suggesting it. The planes are incredible. I could come here every day."

"I'm sure the fly boys would love that."

"What do you mean?"

"Oh come on Angelique, you're like a beacon in that pink gingham dress and your big pink hat and that long blonde hair. They're falling over themselves to give you personal tours."

"Don't be silly. They're amazingly polite to everyone. Including you. And you're pretty cool looking yourself in that yellow dress."

"Thanks. Aren't you tired yet? I'm worn out and I think my feet are bleeding."

"Sorry. I don't want to miss anything. Do you mind checking out one more plane - I'd love to go inside that fighter at the end of the row."

"Sure. We'll have to get moving. The open house is over in half an hour."

"Let's go. There are only four people in line."

In the cockpit the pilot and co-pilot, in their air force blues, are saying goodbye to the last two tourists. The pilot, tall, dark and good looking, shakes Bridget's hand.

"I'm Mark Forrester and this is my co-pilot Jim Hicks. Welcome aboard."

"Nice to meet you both. I'm Bridget and this is Angelique. She's from

Canada and she's nuts about planes."

"Well, let's get started. Jim will give you specifics on the plane's history and function and I'll describe the cockpit and flying."

"Can we sit in the cockpit?"

"Sure can. Great hat." Angelique smiles at him.

BOSTON

"And that's the way it started. The guys invited us to a movie on base. Jim took a shine to me and Mark – your father – was smitten with Angelique."

"So what happened?"

"We all got together whenever the guys flew into Bermuda which was almost every week. We would go dancing, to movies, to the beach or just hang out in a cafe. There was nothing serious and we all became good friends. But Mark was older and probably more mature than we were and his intentions towards Angelique became more serious as time passed."

"And what about her?"

"Angie made no bones about the fact Bermuda was just a stop along the way for her. She had a list of things she wanted to do and places she intended to see. I knew her well enough by this time to know this was not negotiable and she would be leaving sooner or later. Her next stop was England. I don't think your father believed she really would leave."

"Do you think she loved him?"

"I don't really know. She never said. Angelique became very ill about five months after we met Mark and Jim and everything seemed to change. Jim was sent to Vietnam and I never heard from him again. I later heard he was killed near the end of the war. Your father was one of the few people Angelique would see when she was sick and maybe that gave him false hope."

"What was wrong with her?"

"I think that's a story for Angie to tell."

"But she left?"

"Yes. She was barely recovered when she announced she had a one way ticket to London. She was going to work in a theatre in England. I thought Mark would burst into tears but she was so excited I don't think she noticed how distraught he was. It was Sunday afternoon and she was leaving the following Saturday."

"Did they continue to see each other?"

"Only once. Mark took her dancing on Friday night and finally told her how he felt."

BERMUDA – Kindley Officers Club

"I'm going to miss dancing with you. You fly boys sure know how to dance."

"You don't have to go"

"I know, but yes I do. Don't look so serious, you'll find another dance partner."

"I don't want anyone else. Come on let's sit down."

"I'll write when I can. I'm staying with my friend Sue for a few weeks in London then I'll be going to Manchester. That's where I'll be working. Hey. What's wrong? Aren't you happy for me?"

"Yes, of course. No. I'm heartbroken. I want you to stay and come home to the States and marry me."

"You want to marry me?"

"Yes I do. I knew almost from the day we met I would ask you to marry me some day. I'll never forget you coming into the plane that day in your big pink hat."

"My hat! I left it in the hangar when I was waiting for you earlier."

"We'll pick it up on the way off base. So?"

"So?"

"So what do you think?"

"Mark, I've only just turned 19. You're 27. I'm just starting my life and you need someone who wants to settle down, have a family and build a

28

home. I'm not that person and I've never pretended to be."

"I love you Angelique. We have fun together and we have so much in common. We could be happy together."

"I think the world of you. You're the kind of man any girl would want to settle down with. But I can't. I would be terribly unhappy and eventually so would you. I have to move on. I'm really sorry."

"Don't you even want to think about it for a day? An hour? Even a minute?"

"Mark, the answer will still be the same. I can't stay here. I just can't. I'm a mover and I probably won't stay anywhere for a long time. Being so ill these past months made me realize how fragile we all are and I don't want to spend my life regretting."

"You might regret not staying with me?"

"I might. But I still have to go. I'm sorry."

"I'll always love you. Remember that wherever you go. I'll never forget you."

Angelique's eyes fill with tears as she stares across the table and for a split second wonders if she's doing the right thing. Mark breaks the silence.

"Come on, let's go to the Islander for coffee and that chocolate dessert you can't pass up."

In the Islander their conversation, as always, is filled with debate, stories and laughter.

"I'll miss this place."

"That's because they'll play Some Enchanted Evening as often as you ask for it."

"Important reason."

Angelique, checking the time, reaches out and takes Mark's hand.

"I have to go."

"Yes. I know."

"Oh, after this. I love this song."

"Forgive me if I prefer not to listen to someone singing Bye Bye Love."

"OK. Come on. Just walk me to the top of the hill. You can get a cab from there to the base."

"OK."

They slowly walk up the hill and stop to look back one final time at Hamilton Harbour. It was a ritual. They always gaze in awe at the lights reflected in the water and the constant activity even late at night. Mark's arm encircles her slight shoulders. Her illness had made her even slighter. He desperately wishes he could say something to make her stay with him. He wants to be the one who looks after her for the rest of his life. The lump in his throat won't let him to utter a word.

She reaches up and runs a finger over the metal wings on his jacket.

"I may not be able to stay here with you Mark, but I'll never forget you either. I wish things could be different, but I know in my heart they can't be. You are a very special man and special to me."

He tips her chin and lowers his mouth. For him it would have to be a kiss to last a lifetime. To anyone watching the embrace was that of two lovers sealing a future. And it was, just not the kind of future the onlooker would have imagined.

Angelique slowly moves away, her eyes glistening with tears. She could see the agony in Mark's eyes and wishes for a moment she could change her mind. She brushes her finger again across his wings.

"Fly safely." Mark nods and she turns to walk away.

30

"Promise me you'll find me if you ever change your mind?"

"I promise."

At the crest of the hill she turns, stands for a few seconds, lifts a hand to her mouth and sends that air kiss to a broken hearted man. Turning from him for the last time, she disappears down the far slope of the hill. He stands for what seems like an eternity, willing her back. Finally admitting defeat he walks to the cab stand.

BOSTON

"They talked in the Islander until around 4 a.m. They were always doing that. Mark flew over the apartment building around 10 a.m. and Angelique flew out of Bermuda on the 8 p.m. flight to London. They never saw each other again. It was the first Saturday in September. I've never forgotten that day."

"Neither has my father. What about the hat?"

"Angelique forgot to pick up her hat and Mark told me years later that he flew with it in the cockpit of his plane for about seven years, until he met your mother."

"Do you have any photos of her?"

"I have an album filled with photos of the three of us. It broke my heart when Jessie died. She was on her way to marry the love of her life in England and was killed in a car crash after leaving the airport in London. She was a great person who deserved more happiness than she got in life. Excuse me. I'll be right back."

Bridget returned with a large photo album with pages of scenes that told me one thing for sure - Angelique loved to laugh. She had a big smile and Bridget said it was rare to see her sad. She was slender with pale blonde hair almost to her waist. I remarked that in almost every photo she was wearing her pink hat.

"She certainly loved that pink hat. It went everywhere with her. She wore it with whatever she was wearing, no matter if it matched or not. It was like her signature. This is a photo of the day we were at the open house on base, the day we met your father. Oh, here is one with all four of us. Lord, we were young. I have an extra copy of that one, would you like it? It might help when you're asking about her."

"Thank you. I appreciate this. Do you have any idea where we can find Angelique. Here are two addresses Dad tried when he went to England but she wasn't at either. She'd moved."

"She did a lot of moving. I lost track of her a number of years ago, but I do have a couple of addresses you might try if you go to England. This one is on Barrington Road in a town called Altrincham - I'm not sure of the address - and a later one in a nursing residence in Wythenshawe, just outside Manchester. She described the house on Barrington Road as an old English manor house and said she and several acting students rented rooms on the second floor. I also have several names of friends she mentioned who might help you if you can find them. These are acting friends. Jean Taunton and Helen Harrison. Call the Garrick Theatre or the Library Theatre and someone there might know where they are. This woman, Florence O'Connor, is an Irish nurse. You might find her through the Manchester Royal Infirmary where they worked together. I'm afraid that's all I have."

"I can't thank you enough."

"Oh. There was another place she often mentioned in her early letters. Knutsford. That's where she lived with an English family. She loved it there. But I can't imagine you'll find anyone there who would know her after so many years. Do me a favour - If you can, please let me know if you find Angelique. We were great friends. I've never forgotten her. Now, let's eat. You must both be starved. I am. I've prepared a seafood casserole, my specialty."

Flying back to Lompoc early the next morning Paul and I dissect Bridget's information. In his practical way Paul wonders if we shouldn't try calling the Manchester hospital and theatres before hoping on a plane to Europe. Agreeing it would save us time, we decide to make the calls before we saw Dad again.

Our first call was to the human resources department at the Manchester Royal Infirmary. The woman on the line listened to Paul then firmly explained they did not give out employee information over the phone to strangers. We tried several times to speak to a live person at the theatre Bridget told us about, with no success. And no one returned our calls.

It was clear we were going to have to go to England if we had any hope of tracking down Angelique's friends and hopefully Angelique.

LOMPOC

Dad did not look well but was in good spirits and was delighted Bridget had been able to give us a few, but unfortunately, slim leads.

"Dad do you have a photo of Angelique?"
He hesitates.

"Yes. I have one taken the day we met. It has all four of us in it. Jim, my co-pilot, and Angelique and Bridget. I put it in the trunk and never looked at it again after I met your mother. I somehow felt it would be a betrayal. But I couldn't get rid of it."

"Like this one? Bridget gave it to us."

His hand trembles as he reaches for the photo.

"That's the way we were. See her smiling. She was always smiling. That's the thing I remember most about her. And her kindness. She was always kind. Told me it was something she learned from her mother. So what happens now?"

"Now Angeline and I head to England. We fly home tomorrow to see David and get him settled at my sister's, then we'll try to book tickets to England for the weekend."

Dad nods and closes his eyes.

"Dad. Are you OK? What's wrong?"

"I'm sorry. You must think me a silly old fool. Perhaps we should call this search off and let me just live with a memory. What if she doesn't want to see me? or even remembers me. Do I want to be intruding into her life? This is beginning to feel like a very selfish quest."

"Dad, this is important to you. And if she doesn't want to see you - well, we'll cross that bridge when we come to it. I have to admit I found it a bit bizarre at first. You know, trying to find a woman my father loved before he married my mother and wanting to find her now that my mother is dead. But after talking to Bridget in Boston I have to admit I'm intrigued by it all myself and I'd like to meet this woman who has had this effect on you."

"I really don't want to cause Angelique grief over this and I'm not doing it because I hope she'll fall into my arms. She has to understand that. There is just a wound inside me that's never healed and in some strange way I feel I need to see her one last time. It's as if I need it to close the loop on my life."

"I understand Dad. You concentrate on getting well. Paul and I will do everything we can to find her. We'll deal with everything else when the time comes. Get some sleep. I'll call you before we leave."

"Paul, thank you."

"No problem Mark. You take it easy and don't be stressing over this. It will all work out."

"Love you Dad."

"Love you too Angel. Be safe."

Home in Texas, Paul and I spend several hours planning a strategy. We decide to fly directly to Manchester airport and stay at a bed and breakfast in nearby Altrincham.

"What if we don't find her? Dad will be so disappointed."

"We don't know what's going to happen. Let's hope for the best outcome, whatever that is."

"You're right. I guess. You know dad has never asked me for anything. Absolutely nothing. Not even to help pay any of the money he spent sending me to school. I really want to do this one thing he's asked me to do, even if it is a pretty bizarre request."

"And you will. We will do everything we possibly can to track Angelique down. That's all we can do. I've been thinking that if mom had not died we wouldn't be doing this."

"That's true. But, here we are."

"Yeah. I feel badly about us not..."

"We'll work that out as well. There's plenty of time."

"You're a good man, Paul Winterton."

"Yeah, I know. Get some sleep. I'll try to book our tickets online. See you for breakfast."

He kisses her on the forehead. She leans in to him. They slowly move away from each other.

MANCHESTER, England

The cool, bright May day that greets us in Manchester is exactly what I'd imagined England to feel like. Hailing a cab we head to the Olde Manor Bed & Breakfast on Barrington Road in Altrincham. Stepping out of the cab I am drawn to the elegance of the old but beautifully kept manor house. The warm greeting inside from the young woman called Lizzie only added to the overwhelming sense of welcome I was feeling. With an invitation to afternoon tea she showed us our cozy twin-bedded room and left us to "get comfy."

We were staying three nights so I take time to remove clothes from my suitcase and place them in drawers lined with lilac-scented paper. From the eyelet edged bedcover to the copies of Jane Eyre and Wuthering Heights on the book shelf, everything felt so English.

"I love this place. Everything is so charming."

"Well, let's go have the quintessential British afternoon tea."

Five other couples look up as we enter the very English parlour for tea. It's 3:30 p.m. and everyone seems relaxed. If any of them are in a hurry you don't sense it in the room. We are greeted with a warm "hello" or "afternoon" from all of them. Three couples sound English, one French or German and one unmistakingly Scottish.

Pots of tea arrive with small sandwiches without crusts and a plate of scones. Fresh, fabulously thick Devon cream and jam round out the offering. Not having eaten since breakfast, about nine hours before, we were starved and both did justice to even the last crumbs on our plates. The other couples who sat down to eat much earlier left before we finished a first cup of tea.

The friendly Lizzie bustles over to chat as we are on the last cup. She knows we are American from the registration information we'd given her.

"Is this your first visit to the U.K.?"

"It is for me. Paul has been to London on business several times."

"Is this a holiday or business?"

"A bit of both I suppose. We're trying to track down a friend of my father's who came to England many years ago. One of the addresses we have for her is actually on Barrington Road. She lived in a house that sounds like this but it had rented rooms."

"That's interesting. I believe when my grandmother lived in this house she let some of the rooms to help with her finances. She rented to a lot of students who were in school in Manchester."

"Wouldn't it be something if this was the actual house she stayed in? Paul, do you remember anything else Bridget said about the Barrington Road place?"

"She said there were a lot of acting students in it at the time."

"Well, granny kept impeccable records and we still have them. If you like I'll ask mum if she can get them down from the attic and bring them over when she comes in the morning."

"We'd be really grateful if it wouldn't be too much trouble."

"Not at all. Now, I'll get out of your way. There's a map of the town and surrounding areas at the front door. You'll find some interesting shops on the high street and a variety of places to have dinner. See you in the morning. Let me know if there is anything you need."

"Thank you so much."

As we walk along the high street and other streets lined by a mixture of quaint Elizabethan-style cottages, often side by side an industrial revolution row house, I can't help but picture Angelique here. She haunted my childhood and now I want to find her as much for me as for Dad.

"It's strange to be walking these streets knowing the person you're looking for was once here."

"I've been thinking the same thing Paul. Look, there's the Garrick theatre. Let's go in."

The building is undergoing major renovations which, from the before and after pictures, it badly needs. Despite its historical significance in the town, the original theatre building was somewhat drab and nondescript.

The teenager in the theatre office did not remember actors from a previous season let alone from a time before she was born. We explain who we are and why we've stopped in.

"Is there anyone who might remember actors who performed here twenty or thirty years ago?"

"Alice Simpson might. She's an usher and she's been coming to help out for over fifty years. She might know."

"Where can we find her?"

Looking at her watch. "She'll be here in ten or fifteen minutes. She's helping in the office tonight. Would you like to wait?"

"Yes," we say in unison.

As we walk across the room to get a closer look at photos of actors hanging on the far wall the door opens and a slight, energetic woman with a shock of white hair comes in like a gust of wind.

"Lovely evening Barbara. How are you dear?"

Her accent has an aristocratic cadence and it is obvious that Barbara is somewhat Intimidated by her brusk manner.

"Fine, Miss Simpson. And you?"

"Lovely, thank you. Anxious to get started. There's plenty to do around here with the manager off to India for a month. I hope you were able to make some sense out of those receipts I left with you yesterday."

"Yes, I have. Miss Simpson, there's a couple here from America and they'd like to speak with you. Apparently they're looking for a girl who used to act here."

She beckons us over to the desk.
"Mr. and Mrs. Winterton, this is Miss Simpson."

We shake hands. Her tiny hand belies its iron grip.

"Please, call me Alice."

"I'm Angeline and this is Paul."

"What can I do for you?

"We're trying to find Angelique LaPierre. We believe she was an actor here. Do you remember her?"

"Of course. Everyone knew Angelique. A small Canadian girl with a big, happy smile, and talented. She played many roles here. Why are you looking for her? She's been gone a long time."

I explain, giving her a bare bones version.

"Would you know where she might be living now?"

"Oh dear, no. She's lived all over the country and also spent time in several other countries from what I've heard over the years. I have no idea where she is now."

"Well thank you for your time. We appreciate it."

"Wait a moment. I've just had a thought. We have an extensive archive, would you like to see some stills from plays she was in?"

"Yes," we say, again in unison.

The theatre photos are kept in albums, one for every play presented in the theatre. The actors' names are printed on the spine of each album. She finds several with the name Angelique LaPierre.

The first set of photos is from the comedy Barefoot in the Park, a contrast to the dark, sultry Streetcar Named Desire and Shakespeare's Midsummer Night's Dream.

"You see, she played a wide range of roles. I'm sorry I really don't have any more time right now. Have you seen enough?"

"Thank you, yes. You're very kind to take the time."

"No trouble at all. If you're spending any length of time in this area try to see one of our plays. They're very good. I wish you good luck finding Angelique. It's a big world."

Back out on the street we walk quietly for a few blocks.

"Well that last comment really put a damper on our enthusiasm."

"Yeah."

"Let's eat at that Indian restaurant across the street. Curry, I've read, has become England's national dish. The large Immigration of people from India seems to have changed the eating habits of the British."

We linger over dinner, and then stop at a pub near the Manor for a drink. We both know we're delaying the return to our room. Twin beds do not prevent the air of intimacy we are both trying to avoid. The sex was never an issue. We could hardly be in a room alone together without wanting to tear at each other's clothes.

When the inevitable could no longer be delayed we slowly walk back and as we approach the front steps Paul suggests I go on in - he's going to take a walk in the cool night air. I nod. I'm grateful.

I pretend to be asleep when Paul comes into the room. Before he gets into bed he reaches out and gently pushes my hair off my face. It's all I can do to keep from shaking. He gets in his bed and I feel his eyes on me as I fall asleep. Confronting the problems between us might not be far off.

In the morning I get out of bed, quickly shower and dress, wake Paul and head downstairs to the breakfast room. It's 8:30 and Lizzie is bustling around waiting on guests, many I recognize from the previous afternoon tea group. We all wish each other a "good morning."

"Sit wherever you like. Is your husband joining you?"

"Yes. He'll be down shortly. We'll both have the English breakfast."

"Lovely. I'll bring you tea, or would you prefer coffee?"

"Tea is great thanks."

"My mum will be here at 10. She's bringing Gran's ledger books."

"I'll look forward to meeting her."

Paul arrives as Lizzie delivers the tray of tea.

"I've ordered English breakfast. Is that ok for you?"

"When in England..."

"That's what I thought. I couldn't eat it too often but once we've tucked into sausage, potatoes, egg, bacon, ham and toast we won't need to eat until dinner."

"We'll see," Paul says laughing. He knows I'll probably be suggesting we eat again in a couple of hours, being blessed with a wicked metabolism.

Not being rushed, we take more than an hour over breakfast. As we get up to leave the room, Lizzie comes to tell us her mother has arrived earlier than expected and could see us in her office.

Lizzie makes the introductions and Eileen directs us to a couple of chairs.

"Lizzie explained why you're here and asked me to bring these old ledgers. My mother loved having the students here, particularly the acting students. She often wrote detailed notes about them during the time they were here and after they left if she read about them the paper or saw them perform. She also made it easy for us because she listed her tenants alphabetically. Who are you looking for?"

"Angelique LaPierre."

Eileen opens the first of three large ledgers. No Angelique. The second is equally disappointing.

"She may not have been here, you know. Let's look at the last one... oh my goodness, here she is. Angelique LaPierre in room three on the second floor. That's across the landing from your room. It looks like she was here almost a year."

"Does it say where she went after she left here?"

"No. But Mum did make notes about her and the two girls who shared the landing upstairs. It seems she went to see a play in Manchester about two years after they left and all three of them were in it. Apparently one of them, Susan Small, was getting engaged to a guy by the name of Ken Harris and they planned to live in London. She also has a newspaper clipping about Angelique entering the University of South Manchester nursing school and that she would be living in the Newall House residence off Floats Road in Wythenshawe. You might want to try directory assistance to see if there is a Ken Harris in London and take a cab out to Wythenshawe Hospital. Someone there might be able to give you some information. There's another name here Jean Taunton who also seems to be a friend."

"This is really helpful. Thank you for doing for your trouble."

"Not at all. I'm glad to help. I hope you find her. Now, are you comfortable? Is there anything you need?"

"No, thank you. Everything is wonderful. We love it here."

"Excellent. Just ask Lizzie and she'll get anything you want."

Back in our room Paul calls directory assistance and asks for a Ken Harris in London. Mercifully there are only five. He tries all the numbers. People answering the first three calls don't know a Susan Small. The fourth is a voice message asking callers to try again in a fortnight when "Ken and I" will be returning from holiday in Spain. Guess they don't worry about burglars. The fifth number is no longer in service. We make a note to try the fourth number in two weeks.

"Let's go back to the Garrick to see if they know this Jean Taunton."

"Do you have Angelique's photo?"

"In my purse."

At the Garrick we are warmly greeted by Barbara who addresses us like old acquaintances.

"Mr. and Mrs. Winterton, lovely to see you again."

"Nice to see you too Barbara. We were wondering if you might be familiar with the actor Jean Taunton?"

"Her name is familiar. I saw a play she did about five or six years ago. Let me get the album of photos from the play."

She disappears in the direction of the archive room and quickly returns. She turns several pages, stops and begins reading.

"Oh dear."

"What's wrong?"

"Oh dear. There's a newspaper clipping here. It appears she was killed in an accident two years ago. I'm so sorry."

"That's too bad. Thank you again for helping us out."

"Come back any time."

Out on the High Street we look for a place to get coffee. After walking several blocks we find the Hullabaloo, a cafe bistro off Railway Street. We love to people watch so opt to sit at the single outside table. It's modern but the brick shopping courtyard creates an unmistakable Olde English feel.

"I guess the only lead left is the hospital. Everything we've learned so far has not led to anything concrete. Dad may not get his wish."

"It's not over yet. You can't give up that easily. And you don't know what we'll find at the hospital. Let's head there when we've finished. What was the name of the residence where Angelique lived?"

"Newall House."

"We'll start there, and then go to the HR department in the hospital. They might be more willing to give us more information in person than they were over the phone."

"You're right. Thank you Paul. I couldn't do this without you."

"I'm glad I'm here for you Angel. And I'm glad to help your dad but I'm also here for selfish reasons. I'll do whatever it takes to fix the problem between us."

"I want that too Paul, but do you mind if we don't talk about it right now. There will be a time to do that but not today. I'm trying not to get too stressed out about these dead ends we're running into."

We'll get a lead sooner or later. Let's get a cab to the hospital."

Back on High Street it doesn't take long to hail a cab.

"Where to mate?"

"We'd like to go to Newall House off Floats Road at Wythenshawe Hospital."

"Newall House? Are you sure?"

"Yes. Why?"

"I think it's been demolished. There's been a lot a changes over at the hospital."

"Let's go there anyway."

"Right."

The drive to Wythenshawe takes about forty minutes. The English countryside is green and lush and I wish out loud we were in a convertible so that I could see and smell everything around us as we drive past. That idea lands with a thud.
"The drizzle will keep you soaked and most of the smells around here don't attract tourists," the cabbie offered as he began to slow down on Floats Road. "I was right. This is where Newall House used to be. Note, I said used to be."

We stare out at a large parking lot with a sign informing us of its new function "University Hospital of South Manchester staff parking."

"Another dead end."

"Do you want to get out here or is there somewhere else you want to go?"

"No. We'd like to be dropped off at the main entrance, please."

"Right."

While Paul is paying the friendly cabbie I go inside to ask directions to the human resources department. I don't hold out any great hope we'll get much further in our search.

"HR? You'll find it in the Green Zone on the first floor."

Paul and I walk through the modern, spotless corridors. The direction boards show it to be a state of the art hospital with specialties ranging from cardiac surgery to heart and lung transplants.

We find the HR department and explain to the receptionist who we are and why we are there. She asks us to take a seat and disappears through the door of an office behind her desk. Within minutes she is introducing us to the HR director, a tall, attractive redhead in her forties.

"Mr. and Mrs. Winterton, I'm Kendra Livingston. Please come in."

We sit in leather wingback chairs that appear to have been well used over many decades.

"I understand you're trying to find a nurse who worked here many years ago. Angelique LaPierre?"

"Yes. That's right. We understand there are privacy issues but there's a very special reason why we're trying to find her."

Paul sends me a look that says we might as well tell her the story. I give her an abridged version, but one that's enough to gain some sympathy, and it is evident she also finds the whole situation intriguing.

"Let me see what I can tell you." She begins to click her computer mouse and after several minutes finds what she's been looking for.

Angelique was a staff nurse here and left after three years to return to Canada but I'm afraid we do not have an up to date address for her. The note here says a piece of correspondence sent to the address we do have was returned. That was twenty years ago. This might help you. Her next of kin in the U.K. lists a family in Knutsford. Reginald and Isabelle Alderton at 204 Thorneyholme Drive. But that was a very long time ago and I don't know if you'll find them there now."

"It's worth a try. Do you have the name of a classmate called Florence O'Connor?" She searches again.

"Florence O'Connor staffed here for about ten years and then went home to Ireland. She was from a small village in County Cork. I have no address for her. I'm sorry I can't be of more help."

"You've been wonderful and we can't thank you enough. I apologize for taking so much time when we didn't have an appointment. You've been very generous."

"I'm happy to help. Good luck. I hope your quest is successful. It's quite unusual. Good-bye."

We shake hands and I am struck by her kindness. We get a cab from the hospital and head for Knutsford. The cabbie knows the town and its history well and extols its virtues. We need lunch and he insists on dropping us off at the Rose and Crown, a quaint restaurant on King Street which he insists has the best food in town. He was right. We spend more than an hour over a leisurely meal and agree to explore the ancient town before knocking on the door of whoever lives at 204 Thorneyholme Drive.

It's impossible not to feel transported to another time when you walk around this quaint town. The original cobblestones on Church Hill almost draw you to your knees in an attempt to conjure up the past by running ones hands over stones people have been walking on for ten centuries.

Slowly walking back along King Street we browse or stop to buy in almost every shop. We decide to head to a second hand book shop Paul spotted from the cab on our way to lunch. It is almost at the far end of the street and my feet are beginning to hurt. Little do I know it is to be an incredibly fortuitous visit.

The smell of old books assails our nostrils, but not in a bad way. Both being big readers we share a love of old books. It is a magical place. Not much seems to have changed since its founding one hundred and forty-seven years before (according to the plaque outside the entrance). There is no one in sight and we immediately begin to browse the crowded bookshelves. It may be crowded and old but it is also clean, as though the owners have pride and love for this special place.

"Paul, look, a copy of Little Women given to a granddaughter in 1916. God, I love this place."

"Don't get too carried away. We have only so much space in our luggage."

"I wonder where the sales people are."

"Listen, someone's coming."

I look back and, hurrying from a rear door is a woman with the most beautiful porcelain skin I've ever seen. I can't tell her age but she is possibly fifty.

"My apologies. I should have been here to greet you but I was wrapping several packages of books that must be sent by courier to London by 5 p.m. Are you finding what you need?"

"And then some. I was just telling my husband what a wonderful place this is. Are you the owner?"

"Yes, it was passed on to me by my mother who ran it until she died at age eighty-two. It has been passed down through the family for almost one hundred and fifty years. I've been working here since I was not more than ten years old, so I've been here fifth-three years."

"You must have met a lot of interesting people in all those years"

"I have indeed, from all across the world. You know, I've never left England but I feel as though the world has come to me. I ship books all over the globe. You sound as though you're from America."

"Yes, I'm Angeline and this is my husband Paul. We're from Texas."

"I'm Lucie. And what do you think of England? It must seem small. You have so much space in Texas."

"We love it. I think it will be difficult to get Angeline out of the country."

As we chat and laugh with the very lovely Lucie it crosses my mind that if she's been here over fifty years and if Angelique lived here there's a chance she might have shopped in this bookstore. My heart begins to race. I am almost afraid to ask.

"Lucie, we're here in England because we're looking for an old friend of my father's. He isn't well and would like to find her. Would you mind looking at a photograph of her, just in case...?"

"Not at all. Let me see it."

I take out the photo and hand it to her with fingers crossed.

"Oh my gracious. Sure that's the young Canadian girl who lived with the Aldertons many years ago. I remember her very well. She took an odd turn the first time she walked down King Street. The Aldertons were bringing her here because she loved old books."

"What happened?"

"It was very strange, but my mother quite understood her and was intrigued by what had happened."

"Which was...?"

"Well it seems she began to get a headache and kept blinking her eyes very rapidly and telling the Aldertons the street was changing in front of her. She almost fainted dead away and they brought her in here and asked for a glass of water."

"Did she tell you what she was seeing?"

"She was very quiet but Mrs. Alderton said she told them the street had the same stores but the names were different and described exactly what they all looked like. Well, as she was describing the outside of our shop my mother went quite pale and excused herself. She went upstairs and when she returned she was carrying a very large painting covered in an old sheet. She took off the sheet and turned the painting around. It was King Street with our shop right in the middle of the painting and it was exactly the way the young girl described it."

"What was so unusual about that? Perhaps she had seen a copy of the painting."

"Likely not. It was painted by my great grandfather the year he opened the shop and had been in the attic for at least ninety years. My mother showed them the painting and Mrs. Alderton turned white as a ghost and fainted. When she recovered they all went to the Crossed Arms for tea, and a sherry no doubt. They came in here dozens of times after that but no one mentioned that episode. My mother wanted to talk about it so badly but she could sense it was a taboo subject."

"Do the Aldertons still live in Knutsford?"

"Oh gracious no. They moved almost forty years ago. They moved to Sedbergh in Cumbria. It was their favourite holiday spot in the Lake District. So, when they retired they moved up there permanently."

"Did you know what happened to Angelique? The Canadian girl?"

"Oh she lived here for about two years then one day when she was in here buying books she said she was moving into a flat in Altrincham. I really don't know what happened to her after that."

"Lucie, thank you so much for telling us the story."

"I'm afraid it's not a lot and it doesn't bring you any closer to finding her."

"It does save us having to go and knock on doors trying to find the Aldertons; now that we know they've moved."

We count out pounds sterling for the armful of books neither of us could live without and ask Lucie to call us a cab. On the return ride to Altrincham we are like giddy kids telling each other about our special finds. Just as we've done ever since we met. Without acknowledging it, we both know the other is feeling the nostalgia created by an almost magical experience of the moment.

It had been a long and exhausting day and neither of us felt much like dinner. Stretched out on our beds we read until a vice grip drew our eyelids together and we fell into an exhausted sleep. Waking around eight o'clock refreshed, we decide to head to the nearest pub.

Over warmish English beer and excellent wine we plan our next step. It seems logical to head to the Lake District.

"We'll have to go to this town Sedbergh and look for the Aldertons."

"That makes sense and you did say you wish we could visit that part of

England. Why don't we spend another couple of days here, rent a car and plan on at least a week or ten days so that we can see more of the country."

"That's perfect. Perhaps we can also give Ken Harris in London another call when we get back."

"Or, we can go to Ireland first to try and track down nurse Florence O'Connor."

"We could. We need to give this more thought."

"Let's order another round, go back and sleep on it and re-group in the morning."

"I'll drink to that." I feel giddy from the several large glasses of wine. And strangely happier than I've felt in many months.

MONTREAL, Canada

An unbidden tear swells slowly in her green eyes, spills, and races in a rivulet over the foundation on her Gallic cheekbones. Touched with the emotion of the moment, she ignores its defacement.

Looking years younger than the sixty-five she is celebrating, she draws a long breath. Good health makes it easy to hold and control as she effortlessly extinguishes more than six decades of tiny pink candles.

She cuts the massive cake, serving it personally to the one hundred plus guests, many having traveled from three continents to celebrate with her. Her one and only, totally spoiled granddaughter approaches. The lift of a barely wrinkled brow is sufficient to withdraw an offer to help.

"Sorry G-mere. For a moment I forgot to whom I was speaking."

"You're cheeky. When I'm feeble I'll ask for help."

"I won't hold my breath on that one."

"You're cheeky. Didn't I already tell you that?"

"Often. Can I stay with you and G-pere tonight?"

"Why?"

"Our house is full and I've been partying for three days. Turning sixty-five is taking a lot out of me."

"I'm the one turning sixty-five."

"I've been helping you celebrate. Your place is quiet and I could use a bit of nature out in your backyard."

"I suppose you've already asked …"

"He said yes."

"Well, I guess you're coming. You're cheeky."

"Yeah. Dad says I'm just like you."

"He would. We're leaving in half an hour."

"Ok. I'll meet you at your car. Are you letting G-pere drive?"

"Don't let your grandfather hear you talking like that. Have your cheeky tongue ready in half an hour."

How did they grow so fast, she wonders, as she watches her spitting image move through the crowd, talking, laughing and hugging everyone she passes. The swift passage of time still bugs her, as it had since she was eight.

"Are you tired yet, sweetheart?"

Turning, her heart lurches. That old familiar lurch she's felt for almost forty years.

"I'm ready to go home, but don't tell anyone."

"I've been saying your goodnights, just in case."

"Remember when I'd have a fit if you did that?"

"I have scars deeply etched in my memory."

They laugh. He draws her to him and kisses her. Sucking the essence of each other, the way they'd done from their first kiss on a staircase so long ago.

"That went well."

"It was wonderful to see so many old friends. How did you ever find so many?"

"Our grand-daughter and the internet. She's staying the night."

"So I understand. You spoil her."

"Just following your lead, sweetheart."

"No comment."

They drive the ten kilometres home. His hand on her knee. The way they've driven together since they met.

With him all things are bearable, she thinks. Memories of those seventy years she is celebrating threaten to intrude, but she isn't in the mood. Not that there aren't memories to relish, it's just that she has finally learned to enjoy thinking of nothing.

Later, they sit on the patio, sharing a glass of champagne. She could drink a bottle herself, even today.

Close to midnight, still energized, she doesn't want to go inside, but insists Jon take his arthritic hip to bed.

"Did dancing hurt tonight?"

"No." He lies, making her heart lurch again. "Besides no one loves to dance as much as you do. It rubs off. I'll see you upstairs. Keep G-mere company Roni."

"No problem." She gives him a bear hug.

"You hug like your G-mere," he teases, feigning a lack of breathing ability.

"I haven't quite mastered her iron grip," she teases back.

"I'll just have one of those iron grips and a kiss and leave you to gossip."

She stands as he gathers her into his arms, lifts her mouth to his and feels the sensual sweetness of the love they share.

"Maybe you should come up to bed."

"Soon. Play with your laptop so you won't go to sleep." It is a long standing joke between them. He always takes his laptop to bed to surf his favourite car and political websites.

"Wake me if I fall asleep." Laughing, he limps inside.
She watches. Willing away the pain he won't acknowledge because he knows how much she worries about him, not allowing the vestige of a cloud to intrude on her birthday.

"You and G-pere have an amazing relationship. G-mere? Where are you?"

"What? I'm sorry Roni. I worry about that leg of his. I've been trying to get him to the doctor for years."
"I can't imagine one of you without the other."

"That's not a subject I discuss." She sits. "I don't discuss it because I can't imagine it either. It's unthinkable. He is too important to my life."

"Dad says you've had an interesting life."
"That's true."

"Well?"

"Well, what?"

"What about your interesting life?"

"It's a long story."

"I'm not tired."

"You're not seventy."

"Since when do you use the age card?"

"What do you want to know?"

56

"Well. I've been having a hard time at school and I've been getting a bit depressed. Dad said I should talk to you because you went through some hard times when you were not much older than me. If you're tired I understand and I don't want to be dredging up bad memories on your birthday."

"Tell me what's been happening and if I'm still up to it, I'll tell you what happened to me. OK?"

For more than an hour they talk. As she listens to her grand-daughter, she knows she will have to share her tale of survival. Roni needs to understand that life is a gift. A gift too precious to give up or miss out on, even for a single day.

Sitting back in her chair she begins to speak and the present fades away. Cloaked in the past, her memories are close enough to smell. Realities blur and the words pour in a torrent of unleashed emotion, as though she is describing someone else, someone attached to her. Someone she knows intimately.

MONTREAL

A slender 18-year-old girl sits impatiently on a hard bench. She has waist length blonde hair and unusual yellow-green eyes. Her passion is life, particularly the part filled with acting, dancing, travel and people.

She knows the audition on this cold Friday afternoon in a warehouse studio in Montreal could change her life and lead to experiences across the world. She doesn't know that the journey will also, too often, be filled with seemingly impossible challenges.

Sweating, she takes her place on the makeshift stage and waits for the music to start. With its first notes her body sways, she closes her eyes and begins to sing, afraid nothing will come out of her dry, terror-parched throat. Near the end she allows herself to look out at Andre, the man who would determine her future. He is listening. And nodding. A good sign she hopes.

Near the end the music begins to pulse, the beat picks up and she slips into her prepared dance routine. Prepared only as thought in her head. She has no idea what her body is going to do.

The music stops. Andre nods in her direction. She's in.

BERMUDA

Three weeks after that audition she is rehearsing a musical revue show in Bermuda. The dream is unfolding just as she planned it for herself - a little convent educated girl from a village in Newfoundland. Nothing can stop her now, she thinks.

An interview on a local radio station to promote their show adds to her feeling of triumph, and even that led to more success.

"...and before I let you go, what do you plan to do once the show closes at the end of the season?"

"I'll be leaving for England - hopefully for an acting job and who knows what else. There's just so much to do. I'd also like a job like yours."

The host laughs. "Would you now? I'll have to tell my producer. Life's full of opportunities. Thank you Angelique. I'll be back to see your show."

"Great. Thank you. This has been fun."

Three weeks later her interviewer who had confided to her that he had applied for several jobs in England, is offered a radio job in London and Angelique finds herself hosting his midday show.

"It's all in the plan," she tells her roommates. But the plan also comes with a few wrinkles.

Andre, the 60-year-old producer who brought her to Bermuda is outraged and angry at her refusal to live with him in his apartment. Now, he is furious about the radio job. She dares not tell him she has received a firm offer from a theatre company in England and plans to leave Bermuda in eight months. His apartment is next door to Angelique and her roommates and he is becoming a menace. Hardly a day goes by without him beating on their door and cursing Angelique. One evening when she is home alone she hears his door slam and he starts knocking on her door.

"Let me in. I want to talk to you."

Angelique opens the inner door but keeps the screen door latched. "What do you want to talk about?"

"Let me in."

"I'd rather talk this way. You're angry and shouting and I don't want you in the apartment."

"You're a bitch. You should be helping to pay my rent. And how dare you take another job. I hired you and your services belong to me."

"I work for you but you don't own me. The radio job does not interfere with my night job on the show and I need the money."

"I'm warning you. You'll regret this."

"If you threaten me I'll call the police. And stop beating on the door."

"You're a bitch. I'll threaten you anytime I want and I'll do anything I damn well please."

"Stop shouting. You'll disturb the neighbours and they'll have you arrested."

"I don't give a damn about you or the neighbours."

"What the heck is going on over here? Are you OK?" Angelique turns to see a man she figures is in his thirties, wearing jeans with a khaki shirt and well worn cowboy boots.

"I'm ok but I want him to leave."

"Hey mate, leave the girl alone."

"You keep your Aussie nose out of my business. Hey, get your hand off me. I'll get the cops after you."

"Go for it, after you get out of here. If I hear you've been harassing this girl again I'll get the cops myself..."

The unfit sixty year old is no match for a big muscular young Australian. who pushes him away from the door. Andre stomps back into his apartment slamming his door shut.

"Thanks. I was getting frightened. I've never seen him so wild and angry. I'm Angelique."

"I'm Maurice Sheldon. Me and the wife rented the apartment two doors over for a year."

"I'm glad you came over."

"So am I. You should tell the police about this."

"I will if it happens again. I work for him so it's difficult."

"Well, you know where to find me if he gives you any more trouble."

At the show meeting that night Andre is cold but controlled. The cast can sense the added tension between them. No one asks.

Later, driving her moped along the beach road as she does every night after the show, she wonders what she'll do if Andre continues his hostility towards her. But as the cool midnight air rakes her long hair in its wake and chills her exposed skin, she thinks only of the success she is enjoying. She winces at the sharp, stabbing pain from the smallpox vaccination she'd received three days earlier. It was a requirement for travelers to the U.K. She wonders why the site of the Injection feels like a volcano about to erupt.

"Oh I love the smell of Jesse's coffee in the morning. I can't believe how hard I slept. Ummm. This is how coffee should taste. My eye and lips feel weird. I must have slept on them, or something."

Bridget is staring wide eyed. Her "Oh my God" startles Angelique and a coffee stain spreads down her dressing gown. Putting the coffee mug on the kitchen table she runs to the mirror.

She understands why she finds it difficult to close her left eye. It seems to be lying outside the lower lid. The left side of her face has fallen and she looks like two people. One side of her face is normal, the other looks like a Halloween mask.

She begins to cry. Is inconsolable. She cries until her one good eyelid is swollen shut. With the left eye permanently open, she looks even uglier. Bridget takes her by the arm and they sit on the sofa in the living room.

"Angie, what is going on? Did this just happen last night?"

"Well, I've noticed something wrong for the past week but I was hoping it would go away. It's been difficult to put my teeth together when I brush my teeth and last night it was difficult to sing. I think Andre suspects something is wrong but no one else has noticed. My God Bridget what am I going to do?"

"Get away from that mirror. Jesse just took some bread down to Joyce. That woman must eat a loaf a day. I'll go get her."

Jessie, 42, who is a mother figure for the two girls, takes one look at her roommate's deformed face and calls a taxi to get her to the hospital.

They wait for nearly an hour before being called into the doctor's office. Angelique insists that Jesse stay with her. The doctor, an emotionless British man who appears to be in his sixties, takes a look at her face and says "It's Bell's Palsy. The seventh cranial nerve from the brain to the face is damaged. This may get better, chances are it won't get completely better and it could get a lot worse. That's all I can tell you."

Angelique is stunned. She's just turned 19, barely a woman. Now she is grossly deformed. She wants to scream, but says nothing. A lone tear is all that reveals the depths of her despair. She understands, but doesn't. How could this be happening to her?

Jesse asks "How did this happen?"

"Hard to say really. It might have something to do with the long rides she told me she takes every night along the beach road. The cold wind could have damaged the nerve. Stress can sometimes bring it on. She shouldn't have been doing that. It's too bad."

"What should she do? Are there treatments?" The doctor stands up and walks toward the office door.

"Nothing really. Just hope for the best."

Without options and feeling exhausted, Angelique leaves the hospital, Jessie's arm firmly around her slim, drooped shoulders. Her first thought is that she will have to drop out of the production. The comforting Jessie tells her she will get better, that she is young and resilient.

She would remember that day as the best of the next three hundred.

Besides her roommates the only person she allows to see her deformity is her good friend Mark. The U.S. Air Force pilot had become a close and trusted friend. He picks her up, takes her for rides along the coast and they sit in their favourite cafe until she is tired. He refuses to let her dwell on her physical problems and insists on talking about getting well and her future plans, everything to boost her spirits and renew hope.

But the drooping paralysis worsens over the next several days and to add to her misery her body is being savaged by a reaction to the smallpox vaccination, one of the unfortunates who would suffer a severe reaction to the smallpox vaccine.

Each day brings a new horror. One morning she finds clumps of her long hair stuck to the pillow as her hair thins and falls out. Another day saw her outer layer of skin begins to rub off at the merest touch. The site of the vaccination is red with oozing sores. Her entire left arm is a raw swollen mass from her neck to fingertips, disguising its function as a human appendage.

Jesse called the clinic where Angelique had received the vaccination to ask for help. She was told "rest and aspirin and come to pick up a pamphlet with information on it." The information offers nothing more than dire warnings about adverse reactions to smallpox.

The day her teeth begin to crumble hope starts to fade and real terror sets in. Even a crust of bread is enough to cause pieces of a tooth to fracture. Terrified she consumes only liquids and her friends fear for her life as she shrinks from a healthy robust 112-pound teen, to an emaciated 81-pound ill and frightened youngster.

She is inconsolable. She won't allow anyone to tell her mother in Canada. Jessie begs to be allowed to call her parents and tell them what's happening, saying they would never forgive her if anything bad happened. Jessie and Bridget know, as she does, that she could die. When Angelique does call home she makes no mention of the horrors she is dealing with.

Living on her meagre savings and the kindness and encouragement of her roommates, she struggles to keep some semblance of hope alive inside herself. But each day the sight in the mirror is frightening and she is revolted. She ventures out only at night, walking alone with a scarf covering her disfigured face. Tears fall as she passes restaurants and clubs she had so enjoyed but would not now enter and thinks she might never again.

Two months pass and her depression grows. Hope has long faded and life begins to seem meaningless. She grows sicker, always feverish and in constant pain. Her left arm is so swollen it is almost impossible to hold up without a supportive sling made by her roommates. Friends come to visit and she always sits with the disfigured side of her face away from their view to save them and her embarrassment.

At night she has to tape her eye shut to prevent the destruction of her cornea, and eye drops ease its constant dryness. She can sleep only on her right side which starts to ache with the constant punishment.

At times it's difficult for her to agree to see Mark, but he ignores her attempts to suggest he see less of her and more of his friends and other women.

"Why do you keep coming here? I'm a freak and there are hundreds of gorgeous women in this town you could be pursuing. Not that I'm not grateful for this. I am. But I don't want you to waste your time with me."

"Let me be the judge of what's a waste of my time. And it isn't being with you. Your physical problems haven't changed who you are. And I prefer your company to anyone else I know. And as your friend I want to help you through this. You're still beautiful to me Angelique."

"You're a lunatic. But a very nice one. Thank you for being a truly wonderful friend Mark. Oh God, I want to be me again. I really try to be hopeful but ..."

He hands her his handkerchief. "I know you do and I know how hard this is for you. But please, don't stop believing you'll get well again. It may take time but you will get over this."

"Yeah."

Two weeks later Bridget announces that two of her friends would be visiting from Boston. They are physiotherapists, she said, and want a week in the sun and sand of Bermuda. She doesn't mention the fact she has told her friends about her roommate's ordeal and now suspects they are coming to see first-hand the results of Bell's palsy on a young person. They want to learn more about the condition and see this as a golden opportunity. Little do they know the hurt and harm their curiosity will cause Angelique.

Emma and Judy arrive on Friday morning and check into a cottage on the ocean. Late in the evening they come to the apartment to pick up Bridget and hit some of the popular night spots on the island. The object of their curiosity refuses to come out of the bedroom until they are gone.

On Saturday they are invited for lunch and asked to stay for dinner. Their intentions are clear from the instant they are introduced to Angelique, who agrees to join them for dinner.

"We're sorry to hear about your condition. How do you feel? Do you have any sensation at all in your face? Do you wear a patch on your eye at night? Look Emma, the droop is much greater than those we've seen in textbooks."

"And her eye doesn't close at all. I wonder if the smallpox vaccination is affecting it."

Angelique is horrified. She feels like lab rat. Mustering all the dignity she is capable of she answers their questions, finishes her dinner of soup with crackers, then excuses herself and hides in her bedroom. She avoids them during the rest of their visit and Bridget is careful not to inflict any more hurt on her suffering friend. Because of the callous way they've treated Angelique, Bridget is relieved when the pair leaves the island, but the damage to Angelique's psyche by the reaction of the young physiotherapists is profound. She is now convinced that the life she mapped out for herself is over. She would have to live in the shadowy world of the disfigured where adults look in sympathy or revulsion and children point or cry in fear.

Even Mark, with his eternal optimism, cannot console her.

"Angelique, you are scaring me. Please, please, don't give up. You are unbelievably strong and I've been reading about Bell's Palsy. Most of the time people recover. You will recover. It's just taking time, probably because you have to get over the vaccination reaction."

"I know what you're saying Mark. I am trying. I just don't know how to keep sane any more. I haven't seen any improvement. None. I just stay sick and ugly."

She feels badly that she is not able to tell Mark what he wants to hear. She just has nothing positive left inside. When he drops her at her apartment she watches him walk away a very worried soul. But she can't help or fix the emptiness and hopelessness she feels.

One Saturday night when her roommates had gone dancing to one of her favourite haunts, she lies on her bed watching the moonlight flood into her room. There was a time when the brightness of the full moon on the tiny island filled her with a sense of wonderment. Now, her heart has no room for joy. It is a bleak abyss with no hope.

The day before she had gone to the hospital for a re-evaluation of her condition. Removing the bandage covering the site of the smallpox injection, the doctor shakes his head as he cleans the pus that bubbles up from the deep crater exposing the surface of her arm bone. She glances over. The horror of what she sees makes her feel like vomiting. It's as though a blunt knife had been used to gouge out the tissue from the surface, down through the layers of flesh and scraped it away from the bone. He shakes a yellow, sulphur powder into the hole, then covers it with a thick bandage.

He is the same doctor who had diagnosed her Bell's Palsy. She asks piteously what is to become of her and leaves with the same answer he has given her on her other five visits.

"We don't know what will happen. There is nothing we can do. Take painkillers. You may get better. It's difficult to know."

She is only 19 and all she can see ahead is heartache and an early death. She thinks about her family and all those who love her. None of them are aware she had become so ill. Pain and heartbreak cloud her judgment. Deep inside she knows she should let them come for her, but pain can be a terrible, isolating master.

It was now more than four months since the day she was diagnosed. Despair is her constant companion and without hope she decides her fate, making a decision to end her misery. Dear God she thinks, this is not what I want to do, but I have no choice. I cannot go on this way and I do not want to be a burden.

One evening while she is alone in the apartment she rises from her bed and takes paper, a pen and envelopes from a dresser drawer. She writes a note to her mother and family telling them she is sorry for not telling them about her illness and for taking her life. She asks them to pray for her. Then a note to her roommates thanking them for their love and care. Sealing the envelopes, she places them beneath underwear in a drawer. She has decided to jump from the balcony of the apartment building onto the rocky cliff face overlooking Hamilton Harbour.

The decision weighs heavily. She loves life and does not want it to end this way. But she feels trapped. She walks to the dresser. Bending over she leans on her elbows and cradles her face in the palms of her hands.

As she pushes the skin upwards she notices that the affected side of her face becomes level with the right side.

Dear God, she looks almost normal. A sharp object digging into her right elbow brings her out of her reverie. She picks up a sticky tape container lying on the dresser. It has an unusual phosphorescence made from zinc sulphide that causes it to glow in the dark. Bridget had brought the tape back from Boston on one of her trips to see her family. Without thinking or knowing why, she tears off strips and tapes her face from under her chin, across the left side of her face, around her head, down the right side and back under her chin. She does it six more times and is suddenly overcome by an unbearable exhaustion that sends her to the bed. She lies on her right side with the taped side exposed and falls into an exhausted sleep.

Hours later at around 2 a.m. her friends return. Entering the bedroom they all share they are shocked to see a strange glow coming from the bed on the far side of the room. Bridget turns on the light and they run to their friend. Shaking her awake, they want to know what she has on her face. She raises her hand and barely remembers what she has done.

Jessie cradles her face.

"Look the tape pulls your face back into place," she says excitedly. "That's what we have to do. Keep taping it up like this and perhaps it will eventually stay that way. We have to start getting more nutrition into you to help flush out the vaccine toxins. Sound like a plan?"

They all agree. Jessie pours a glass of sherry for all of them to celebrate. The letters beneath the underwear are forgotten.

The next few months are filled with hours of face taping, concocting milk shakes filled with vitamins of all descriptions and massages under warm water for her badly swollen left arm. As the fifth month approaches she begins to feel better and the swelling starts to decrease. Fear kept her from looking in the mirror so she doesn't know the status of her face. But that becomes clear one morning when she begins brushing and is able to put her teeth together.

She runs to the mirror. Her eye has returned to its socket and there is only a mild droop to the left side of her lips. She begins to cry. That brings her friends running into the bathroom where between sobs she is able to make them understand why she is crying. They hold her until the anguish and terror of the past seven months has spent itself and they hug with renewed hope. She is going be fine. They all believe they are part of a miracle.

Jessie pours sherry for the three of them to celebrate. It is a milestone and they all know Angelique has turned a corner. She goes to sleep that night happier than she has been in more than half a year. She wanted to call Mark but decides to wait until morning.

"Hey flyboy, now that you're back on the island you can buy me a celebratory dinner."

"I'm leaving this afternoon but I'll be back on Friday. Dinner on Saturday?"

"Sounds perfect."

"What are we celebrating?"

"I'll tell you when you get here."

"Will I be happy about it?"

"Absolutely. Gotta run. Bye."

"Angie wait!"

On Saturday night she is dressed and waiting. Her roommates and their dates are joining her and Mark to celebrate. It's her first night out in public since the morning she discovered her deformed face.

For Angelique it is a magical night. They have dinner and head to a nightclub in the Princess Hotel to dance. She is still weak but nothing would have stopped her from dancing until she was too tired to stand. Mark watches her like a mother hen until she tells him he can sit at another table if he doesn't cease and desist. It's a struggle but he manages to keep his protective instincts, especially when it comes to

Angelique, under control.

She runs out of steam at around midnight. They say goodnight to her more energetic roommates and slowly walk the three blocks to her apartment. Acutely aware of her fatigue, Mark gathers her in his arms, wanting her to feel his relief and his need to always be there for her. And his need for her. He kisses her gently, lifts his head to look at her then meets her mouth in an explosion of passion that's a combination of relief and wanton desire. Angelique returns his passion. The fire that makes her breasts swell and urges her to press closer to Mark is like nothing her body has ever experienced. Its intensity makes her exhilarated and frightened. Mark's hands find her overheated breasts and her moan of desire shakes them both. In a turmoil and rattled, Angelique pulls her mouth from Mark's and his hands reluctantly leave her breasts and encircle her waist in an attempt to quiet his raging need for her. She begins to babble. It shakes them both. Angelique pulls away slowly.

"You don't have to worry any more. I'm going to be fine. I will never be able to thank you enough. You've been such a wonderful friend. Thank you for walking me home. Why don't you go back to the club. They'll be dancing until 2 a.m."

"The best jive dancer won't be there so I think I'll just go back to the base. Unless you want to invite me in?

Angelique wants so badly to invite him in but her mind throws cold water on her passion. She knows if Mark comes into her apartment and into her bed there will be no going back. She will not leave Bermuda. That might make her happy but it might leave her with too many regrets. She looks up at Mark and sees the naked love and desire he has for her, but her heart loses the battle.

I'll take your silence as a no. I'll call you tomorrow."

"Not before noon. Goodnight."

"'nite Angie." He turns to leave. "Angie...I...Nothing. I'm so glad you're getting well."

"Thanks. 'nite."

Climbing into bed she wonders what Mark was going to say to her. He seemed preoccupied during the evening and she often caught him staring at her with a strange look on his face. She decides she is too tired to try figuring it out tonight. She rarely sleeps but that night she falls into a contented coma for almost eight hours. It is the longest sleep she's had since getting the nearly fatal smallpox vaccination.

Joyce invites all of them to join her for dinner Sunday night and once again she feels everyone is revelling in the progress she is making. Everyone wants to take a little of the credit for making it happen and she is deeply touched by the depth of their caring. She also notices that while Mark is his usual happy and entertaining self she can't help feeling there is something wrong. But no matter how many times she asks he insists there is nothing wrong and that she is becoming obsessive. She stops asking.

Although she had written several letters to her parents during the past months she had not told them about her illness. Now that she was getting well she finally let them know she had been sick, leaving out the most distressing details. They beg her to come home but eventually tell her they understand her need to continue her journey. Her health and optimism return and she calls to tell them she would be leaving for England within a few months. Three months later she is well enough to travel. The morning she starts packing she finds the letters she'd written in despair, forgotten beneath the underwear in her drawer. The discovery shocks her.

She hesitates, takes the envelopes from the drawer and sits on her bed. She opens and reads each one then rips them into tiny pieces.

In that moment she vows never again to let anything or anyone in her life send her to the brink of ending it. She thanks God for giving her another chance to live and promises herself she will embrace life and love it with all her heart until the day she dies of old age.

The most difficult part of leaving Bermuda is saying good-bye to her friends, especially Mark. He does not want her to leave and the hurt he is feeling makes her question her decision, but only for a moment. She knows she is doing the right thing for her and her future. He is a special person in her life but it would be wrong to give him false hope because there is nothing anyone can say to make her change her mind. Bidding her friends goodbye on a warm Saturday evening she boards a British Overseas Airways Corporation jet and sets out to live the rest of her life.

She never saw Mark or her Bermuda friends again.

MONTREAL

"And so, Roni, now you know."

She looks across at her granddaughter who cannot speak because of the lump in her throat and the tears threatening to spill down her cheeks.

"I didn't mean to make you cry. This has a happy ending."

"Was that really you G-mere? Oh God, what you must have suffered."

"It was a long time ago and that suffering helped make me a better person. It also helped me realize that nothing in life comes easy but things that are worthwhile are worth working for. We always have so much to be thankful for."

"I've been a real pain in the rear. I don't know Mom and Dad can stand to have me around."

"Here, blow your nose. Surely you must realize now that it's never too late. Nothing is ever too late. Life is all about learning and moving forward. Use the past to learn from."

"I think I'll go to bed. Do you mind G-mere? I need to be by myself."

"Are you staying for breakfast?"

"I wouldn't miss the breakfast you two cook up for anything. Good night." She hugs her grandmother.

"I love you so much. Thank you. I'll never forget. Not as long as I live. Ah...do you ever miss your 'flyboy?'"

"Roni!"

"Got it. I'm gone."

She walks slowly into their bedroom, quietly undresses and gets into bed, trying not to disturb Jon.

"How did it go?"

"I thought you'd be asleep by now."

"Couldn't. Wanted to know how she reacted."

"She cried. I think it's given her something to think about in her own life."

"Her father will be grateful."

"To say nothing of her mother."

"You're really something you know? I love you sweetheart."
"And I love you my darling."

"Come on let's spoon." He turns on his left side and opens his arms. I flip over, turning my back to him so that he can pull me into the curve of his body.

As he envelopes her in the safety of his body she holds his gentle fingers in her own. She presses them to her once ruined cheek. She smiles. Then sleeps.

NORTHERN ENGLAND

Paul and I are silent on the journey north on the M6 Motorway into the Lake District. We are both absorbed in thought and ever mindful of the oddity of driving on the opposite side of the road and sitting in reversed seats.

Even along a major highway the countryside is lush and green, but, it's not surprising given the annual rainfall in the country. Two hours north of Manchester we pull off at one of the service centres for coffee.

"You're very quiet. Are you worried about this trip?"

"No. Yes. Sometimes this feels like a great adventure, other times it's like a bad dream. I've been asking myself what the hell are we doing, chasing around the globe to find a woman who might be really pissed off when we find her. If we even find her."

"That's the risk we're taking. We can always turn back. You say the word. If this gets too stressful for you we can fly home and tell your father we couldn't find her. You know he'll understand."

"I know. But if he dies I'll never forgive myself for not doing everything possible to carry out his last request to me. Shit. I hate that pink hat."

We both laugh and the laughter is like a balm. Paul pays for coffee and scones.

"Let's get this show on the road. I want to get this over and get that pink hat out of my life. How much longer?"

Paul checks the map.

"We'll be in a place called Kendal in about three hours. We'll find a bed and breakfast then drive to Cumbria in the morning."

"I think we should we call the Aldertons before we go knocking on their door. Just tell them who we are and ask if we could come to talk with them."

"I don't know. Let's make that decision in the morning."

The winding, narrow roads in the Lake District require great concentration. Not far into the town we book into a twin-bedded room in a picture perfect bed and breakfast. The Olde England charm is echoed in the courtesy of the man and woman at the check-in desk. They take our contact information and make us feel like long lost relatives, delighting in our accents and welcoming us in a way so many Americans no longer experience.

"You're going to Sedbergh? Oh, you'll love it there. It's still very much like it looked in the 16th century. We'll prepare a list of some of the places you should visit and have it ready for you in the morning. And if you're looking for a lovely place for an evening meal here in Kendal we'd recommend the Rainbow Tavern or the Infusion. They're both in walking distance and both have excellent food and service. Just leave your car outside. Breakfast is from 6 a.m. to 11 a.m. Enjoy your stay."

That evening's meal was excellent and the service delivered with the English charm we'd experienced since landing at Manchester airport. Later, in our bedroom, I pull back the curtains and stand looking out across the meticulously kept flower gardens in the back yard. I suddenly feel Paul's arms around my shoulders pulling me into his body. For a moment I allow myself the joy and sudden stirring that always comes with his touch. As if sensing my acquiescence Paul tightens his hold but then kisses me on the top of my head and walks to his bed.

I look back questioningly.

"There is nothing I want more in the world than to have you share my heart and my bed again but I don't want it to happen because of your vulnerability. You've said there is a lot we need to talk about and we do. Until we clear the air between us I won't jeopardize the rest of our lives together. I need you in my life Angeline."

One part of me badly wants to go and lie next to him but I know he's right and all the reasons for this tension between us will be there in the morning. I crawl under the green and white cotton sheets in my own bed.

After breakfast, armed with an extensive list of places we "can't possibly afford to miss" we set out for Sedbergh, having opted to do a cold call on the Aldertons. We aren't sure if it's the best approach but it's the one we decide to take.

As we drive further into the Lake District the English countryside forges an indelible imprint. The miles of green hills dotted with grazing sheep are divided by ancient dry stone walls which we later learn is a dying art, but one some are trying to preserve. I fight a compulsion to get out and run over the hills. The opening scene in the Sound of Music suddenly has new meaning for me, even though Maria was in Austria.

"People are so lucky to live in this place. I can't imagine ever wanting to move away from it."

"Visitors probably say that about many places they visit, at least the beautiful places."

"Maybe. But I can tell you this takes my breath away."

"Here's the Sedbergh sign, three miles."

I begin to get cold feet and question the sanity of just dropping in on people we don't know asking about a woman we don't know and who may not want us to know. Calming my nerves I take out the address we'd taken from a torn and filthy phone book in a phone booth outside Kendal.

"We're looking for 58 Queen's Way. Look, there it is. Queen's Way."

We pull up in front of the two-story brick house and sit there for a few moments. Paul gets out first.

"Come on. Might as well get it over." He walks up the driveway and pushes the bell. The door opens and a young woman gives Paul a broad smile. It can't be Mrs. Alderton because she'd be all of ninety years old. I quickly join Paul on the door step. We introduce ourselves and explain we are looking for the Aldertons.

The woman, who introduces herself as Jill Stockton, frowns.

"I'm so sorry. We bought this house from the Alderton family. I'm afraid the Aldertons are both passed on. I'm terribly sorry to be the one to give you the news."

For a moment we are both too stunned to respond."

"Would you like to come in? I'll make you a cup of tea. You've come a long way."

Over tea and biscuits in her comfortable home, Jill tells us the history of Sedbergh and as we are about to leave she suggests we might want to speak with one of the Alderton children who lives in Scotland. She has an address.

We say goodbye to the affable Jill and drive away. On the main street in the village Paul pulls into a parking spot outside a pub called The Dalesman.

"I need a beer."

While Paul gulps his beer and I sip on cider we discuss driving to Scotland.

"What do you think, should we go to Scotland?"

"Nothing is easy on this damn quest. I dread to think where Scotland will lead us, probably freaking Timbuktu. Maybe this is a sign we should just give it up and head home. This is beginning to feel like a freaking maze. I'm getting freaking tired of being freaking redirected."

I take a very big swig of the cider.

"I'll take that as a no." Paul puts down his drained beer mug. He raises one dark eyebrow and looks at me with a query in the one eye.

I can't stop myself. I begin to laugh. Within moments we are both almost in tears with the giddiness that assails us. We laugh so hard patrons around us begin laughing at and then with us. It doesn't matter they don't know why. There is something companionable and cathartic about shared laughter. The oldest patron insists on buying a round for the house, about a dozen or so jovial souls.

By the time we've shared another three rounds with the publican and his regulars we decide to explore the Scottish hills and in the process try to find Katherine Alderton Lessing, the only daughter of the late Aldertons.

A cool breeze drifting in the window jolts me awake at around 9:30 a.m. I turn and see Paul still sound asleep. Knowing his consumption of English ale the night before I decide to let him sleep.

I sit up and for allow myself to look at the sleeping man with whom I have already shared so much of my life. I know I love him but there is a lump of something that's sticking in my heart and weighing me down. I want to reach across and run my hand down the stubble along his chin, as I often did in the morning when I got up to go for an early run. I resist the impulse, get out of bed, rummage in the suitcase for my dressing gown and head for the shower.

By the time my ministrations are complete Paul is awake. He looks rough.

"Remind me to take aspirin before I go to bed after a night trying to keep up with the Brits. They have amazing constitutions."

"It's how they won the war."

"Didn't we help out?"

"Want breakfast?"

"Not yet. Give me a few minutes and we'll go to that little tea room you said you liked the look of yesterday. I have to admit I'm acquiring a taste for tea and scones. I suppose you can get scones in the morning."

"You can always use your charm on a poor unsuspecting waitress."

"You know where I'd prefer to use my charm. No violence. I'm going."

Three hours later we cross the border into Scotland and head to Dumfries. We decide to find the street where Katherine Alderton lives then spend the rest of the day travelling around the countryside.

We check in to yet another lovely bed and breakfast, the Ferinstosh Guest House, around 6 p.m. I'm becoming a big fan of the B & B and wish there were more of them in the U.S. We decide on a fish and chip meal and turn in by 11 p.m. Paul is still reading when I turn out the light and burrow into my pillow on my side of the bed. No need to tempt fate.

We linger over breakfast and set out to visit Katherine Alderton. My heart races as we pull into her driveway.

"I'm terrified."

"Of what?"

"That she'll think we're nuts. That she'll tell us to get lost. That she'll tell us she hated Angelique and doesn't want to talk about her. That she'll tell us she never met her. I could go on."

"Don't. Let's go knock on her door before you're so terrified you'll want to drive off. We've come too far to turn back now."

The English are so darn polite. Here we are - knocking on a strange woman's door, telling her a fanciful tale and she just smiles, introduces herself, welcomes us to Scotland and asks us in for tea to discuss our enquiry.

Over tea we explain the quest we've agreed to and try to make it sound normal for a grown daughter and her husband to leave their teenage son to wander around the globe looking for her widowed father's lost love.

She nods and smiles in all the appropriate places.

"You must love your father very much. This can't be easy for you. But you want to know what I know about Angelique. She lived with us for more than a year after she left London. She rented the upper loft of our house but she spent most of her time downstairs with us. She used to tire easily and often fall asleep in the big old armchair by the window. She suffered from several health problems when she lived in Bermuda and it took a year before she felt really healthy. She was part of our family and we were sorry to see her leave when she decided to take a flat closer to the theatre where she worked."

"Did you keep in touch with her after she left?"

"She kept in touch with Mum and Dad. They were very close. But I don't think they saw as much of her after she went to nursing school. Then they came north to Sedbergh and she went to Paris to work for a year. After she came back she used to visit every couple of months for a few years. Then she went back to work on the continent. Spain I think."

"Are you saying she's living in Spain now?"

"Oh no, that was decades ago. I don't know the details of what she was doing but from what I understand from Mum and Dad she came back to England after Spain and was employed doing voiceover work at BBC Radio for about six months, then was a staff nurse at the Manchester Royal Infirmary for about a year."

"So she's still in England?"

"I'm afraid not."

"Where is she? Do you have any idea?"

"I'm sorry. I don't. But I can check with my brother in Athens. He's kept in touch with her all these years and I seem to recall him saying she had left Europe."

"I don't mean to be pushy but how soon do you think you could check with him?"

"I'll call him tonight and will hopefully have an answer for you tomorrow. Are you staying in Dumfries tonight?"

"Yes. We're checked in to a bed and breakfast about two or three miles from here."

"That would be the Ferintosh."

"Yes. It's lovely. We should be going. I can't tell you how much I appreciate your help. I'm not sure if Dad knew how challenging this quest of his would be."

"Perhaps he did but he must have faith in your tenacity to find Angelique."

"Maybe. Do you want me to call you tomorrow?"

"Yes, that would be better. Call in the morning after 11."

"I will. Thank you Katherine."

"Enjoy your evening."

As we'd be doing a lot since we arrived in the United Kingdom, we headed to the nearest pub. "When in Rome, do as the Romans," Paul keeps telling me as I am led into one pub after another.

"You look irritated. And tired."

"I am tired Paul. I hope this lead goes somewhere. I need something positive to happen for a change, not just another recommendation to look somewhere else."

"Katherine's brother sounds promising. If he's been keeping in touch with Angelique it might be our strongest lead yet. So don't get discouraged until we talk to her in the morning. Want to take a walk around the town?"

"Sure. I need to get rid of the cobwebs. And we need to call our son. The last time we talked to David he must have asked me five times when we're coming home. I think he misses us."

"He's probably finding it hard to compete with all his cousins and my sister's house is like grand central station. Our son will have a whole new appreciation for his own room."

"Yeah. Being an only child isn't all bad."

After spending almost four hours walking around the picturesque Scottish town exploring the castles, shops and scenery and drinking in a two hundred and fifty-year-old pub, we head back to the B & B to call David.

"Mom, when are you coming home?"

"Hopefully by the weekend. How are you darling?"

"I'm ok. I'd like to go home. Aunt Janice is great but I'd like to be in my own place."

"I know. We're looking forward to getting back to our own place too. Here's your dad."

"How's it going son? Need a break from your cousins?"

"Yeah. I mean no. You know what I mean?"

"I think I do. We'll be home in a few days. Hang tight."

"Hey Dad. What happens if you don't find that woman?"

"I don't know son. We'll cross that bridge when we come to it. Let's hope we get lucky. Your mom says she loves you."

"I love her too. You too Dad."

"I love you too, David. See you in a few days."

"Imagine, our son missing us! You looked wiped." He puts his arms around her. "Why don't you turn in. I'm going to spend some time with a book I saw in the sitting room."

"Ok. See you in the morning."

Even though I am mentally and physically exhausted I find it difficult to sleep. My mind keeps going over everything we've done so far, every person we've met and I keep wondering if there is something we've missed. I'm afraid to hope that Katherine's brother will tell us where to find the elusive Angelique.

I hear Paul's key in the door and close my eyes. Before he gets in bed I sense him near me and as he has done many nights when I've gone to bed before him, he brushes back my hair and I feel his lips on my forehead. Oh God. I have an urge to reach up and pull him down on the bed with me. I make myself breathe evenly. He sighs and slowly moves away.

Then I begin to think about Paul and me and wonder how or if we'll be able to bridge the rift between us. There have been so many times in the past couple of weeks when I wanted to be able to lie next to him at night and feel comforted in his arms. But I know that would just make me feel good for the moment but wouldn't fix whatever is ailing in our relationship.

In the morning I'm so nervous I can hardly swallow my boiled eggs. While waiting for the clock to tell us to call Katherine I try to read a magazine but soon realize I keep reading the same lines over and over. I begin a countdown from 10:15.

"It's eleven. Do you want to make the call?"

"No. You do it. I'm afraid to ask her."

"Katherine. It's Paul. How are you?"

"Just fine Paul. How is your wife?"

"She's fine. Anxious." He laughs at whatever it is she is saying.

"Were you able to reach your brother? Oh yes. I see. That's too bad."

Angeline gets more despondent with every utterance.

"What? What?" she mouths.

"Oh really? Yes, I do. One moment. Angel, a pen?"

Angeline takes a pen out of her purse and watches Paul write down a phone number.

"Katherine, I don't know how to thank you. We're so grateful for your help. Yes, I will. Good-bye."

"So where is she? We've got her number? I can't believe it. Oh my God. I can't believe it. So where do we go now?"

"Well, we go home."

"What?"

"We don't have Angelique's phone number?"

"Then whose is it?"

"Katherine's brother Simon. He wants us to call him after we return to the U.S. He wants to call Angelique himself to ask if he can give us her contact information."

"Damn it. Not again. I can't freaking believe it. We were so close. Now we're going back with nothing. Damn it. Damn it. We'll go all the way back to the States and will have to come here again if that damn woman agrees to see us." She starts to cry in anger and disappointment.

"Angel. Angel. Listen to me. We are close. Simon told Katherine Angelique is living in Canada. She lives in Montreal. Simon just wants to make sure she is comfortable with him giving her phone number to a couple of strangers. Let's go find a travel agent and arrange to go home. The sooner we get back the sooner we can call Simon. I have a good feeling she will agree to see us."

"You're right. Let's go. I'll be glad to get home."

The travel agent finds a flight for us from Manchester to Dallas that's routed through Detroit. We have two days and decide to head to Manchester to see something of the city before flying home. Somewhat mollified by Paul's logic I try to get in a more upbeat mood on the drive south but it's a struggle. The estrangement between us, the frustration and tension of the hunt we were on and the ambivalence I was experiencing most nights about Paul was fraying my nerves and I feel worn out.

My mood isn't lost on Paul. He pulls into the slower lane of traffic.

"Want to talk about it?"

"About what?"

"Whatever has you in a serious funk. We're closer to finding Angelique than any time since we started this running around the world. So what's the problem?"

Something in the tone of his voice sets me off.

"Look if you're trying to tell me something just say it. It's typical of you to half say something and not say what you really mean. Just be honest and say it."

"What's got in to you? I'm not trying to say anything. You're overwrought. Why don't you try to have a nap for an hour or so. Maybe it'll make you feel better."

"I don't want to sleep I want you to talk, damn it. Just tell me what's on your mind."

"What do you want me to talk about? It seems you're the one who wants to talk so why don't you start talking and let's get this over. I don't want this tension between us. I want us to be the way we were. We have a minor argument about something so stupid I don't even remember what it was and suddenly you want out and we're living like brother and sister. So no, I don't want to talk because I don't know what to talk about."

"Why would you, everything is always about you. We make decisions based on what's best for you. Whether it's which city to live in, what kind of house to buy where to go on holiday, the kind of furniture to buy the colour of carpets and on and on. It's all about you."

"You're being very unfair. You know that's not true. We make decisions together, at least it's always seemed that way."

"Did you give me a chance to say no when you wanted to take that job in Dallas? Did you ask if I wanted to live in Dallas? Did you ask if I minded giving up my job in New York, a job I worked so hard for? Did you ask if I wanted to leave New York? No, you took it for granted, just assumed that because you were offered a great job I should be happy to pull up my life and follow you, whether I liked it or not. All that was important was for you to have a great opportunity. To hell with me and my career."

"Angel, do you really believe what you're saying? We discussed leaving New York and talked for days about my taking the job in Dallas. You never once told me you didn't want to live in Dallas. "

"Would it have done any good? This was the job that was going to set you on a career path, the opportunity you'd been waiting for and on and on. What was I going to say? That I was going to keep you from your opportunity of a lifetime? Yeah, that would have gone down well. Was I going to say no, I'm staying in New York, that's where my opportunities are and where my career path lies? And what would you have said, that you understand, that you'd give up the job in Dallas to let me have my dream? Not likely."

"I wish you had told me how you really felt. How could I know what you wanted if you didn't tell me? I can't read minds. And where do you get off making assumptions about what I would or wouldn't do? Of course I would have to know what I was making a decision about, which I didn't because you weren't honest enough to tell me the truth about what you didn't want. That's damned unfair and I can't believe you've been harbouring this resentment ever since we've been married. Talk about living a lie."

86

"You're a bastard. You're turning this on me and it's you. You're the one who has to be the most important person in this marriage. I couldn't even choose the hospital where I'd be giving birth."

"Now you're being ridiculous. I suggested St. Mark's because it's the most modern hospital in Texas. You seemed happy with the choice, now you say you didn't want to go there? You've said nothing for fourteen years?" Tears that have been threatening for weeks spill over.

"You don't get it do you? You don't understand how hard this has been on me. And you obviously don't care."

"Angel, please don't cry. I told you I didn't know you felt this way. If you had told me we could have worked something out, something that would work for both of us. I love you Angel. Your happiness is more important to me than any job. Our life together is more important."

"Paul, watch out. Oh my God." There is a loud bang, a flash of dark green and the sound of crunching metal as a green van crumples the front of our car. Then nothing.

Angeline slowly opens her eyes. She is lying on a stretcher in an ambulance. She hurts all over. An oxygen mask covers her mouth and clear liquid is dripping into a vein from a bag hanging on a pole. She looks around, trying to see if Paul is with her in the ambulance. She whimpers and a paramedic tries to soothe her. She doesn't want soothing; she wants to know where Paul is. She tries to ask but the words won't come out. She closes her eyes and when she opens them again she is in a hospital bed.

"Mrs. Winterton. How do you feel? Can you squeeze my hand? Good. Would you like to take off the oxygen mask? OK"

"Where's my husband? Where's Paul?"

"I'm going to send Dr. Erikson in to talk to you. He's just at the nurses' station.

"What's wrong? What's happened to Paul?"

"Please don't get upset. Let me get the doctor."

She leaves and soon returns with a tall, blond doctor who looks about thirty years old.

"Hello Mrs. Winterton I'm Dr. Dan Erikson. How are you feeling? You have no serious injuries but you did get a severe bouncing and some bad bruising that will take some weeks to heal."

"I hurt all over but I feel OK. Where's my husband?"

"He's in surgery. He suffered extensive internal organ damage but we won't know how extensive until they've taken a good look inside his abdomen. He also has a fractured left femur."

"What happened? I saw a van coming into our lane and heard a crash, then nothing."

"The driver of the other car appeared to lose control of his vehicle and crossed the median, coming into your lane and hitting your car head on."

"What happened to the other driver?"

"Unfortunately his injuries were so serious we couldn't do anything to save him. The police are having his van checked out to determine why the airbag didn't deploy."

"Oh my God. When will Paul be out of surgery?"

"They've had him in there just over three hours. I'll go check. Please try to get some sleep."

My guilt made sleep impossible. If I had not started our argument Paul might have been more attentive to his driving. He had told me it took a lot of concentration for him because he wasn't used to driving on the left hand side of the road. Maybe if I had waiting to have that fight until we were out of the car he would not be fighting for his life and another man would not be dead. A man who has probably left behind a grieving family.

I begin to think about what Paul had said. He was right, I didn't tell him what I really thought. I let him believe I was happy and supportive about his job and our move to Texas. I made the decision not to tell him I wanted to stay in New York. It seemed like the right thing to do at the time. And living in Dallas wasn't so bad, except for the fact I had not found a job I liked as much as my job in New York. Now that I was being honest with myself I begin to realize that I never found the perfect job because I didn't think it existed in Texas. It wasn't New York so I never really let myself be open to other possibilities.

If I had been open and honest about my feelings all of this might not have happened. Mercifully, the morphine in the IV drip banishes my ability to think and I fall into a healing sleep.

 I wake to the sound of a nurse's voice asking me to open my eyes. She wants to check my vital signs. I am fine.

"My husband?"

"He's in ICU. He's doing well. The doctor will be along in a few minutes to talk to you."

She removes the IV and suggests I might like to take a shower before breakfast. All I really want is to see Paul. The doctor is waiting when I come out of the bathroom.

"Mrs. Winterton, you look much better. How do you feel?"

"I'm fine. Can I see Paul?"

"Yes, of course. He had a ruptured liver and a punctured lung and a lot of internal bleeding but he's going to be fine. Come with me.

As I walk into the ICU I see Paul on his hospital bed looking like a ghost shrouded with tubes. Moving to his bedside I pick up his hand and hold it to my lips. His eyes flicker and he squeezes my fingers. I don't think I have ever loved him as much as I do in that moment. Knowing how close I came to losing him makes my behaviour over the past few months seem so futile and petty. I lean over to kiss his forehead.

"I love you Paul. Just get well so we can go home." He does not respond and the doctor indicates for me to follow him from the room.

"We have to keep him very quiet for a few days so we're keeping him heavily sedated. The next forty-eight hours will be critical. After that I expect him to make good progress."

"How long before he can travel?"

"I would say about two weeks at least. You'll need a place to stay so I've taken the liberty of asking my assistant Beth Murphy to book you into a bed and breakfast close to the hospital. She will take you there and help you get settled. In the meantime, if you need to call your family in America there's a private phone box you can use just outside the nursing office."

"Thank you. I would like to make that call now."

"This way. Once you have finished go to the nursing desk and ask for Beth. She'll help you out from there."

"Thank you. I appreciate everything you're doing for us."

"Think nothing of it. Please let us know if there's anything you need."

Sitting in the small phone booth I try to collect my thoughts to put together what I'm going to tell Janice so that she doesn't panic and worry David. I dial and David answers.

"Mom. When are you coming home?"

"We've been delayed for another week or so. I'm sorry darling I thought we'd be home sooner. We had an accident and your dad was injured. But he's going to be fine."

"An accident? How? What happened? Are you OK?"

"Yes, I'm fine. We were hit head on by an out of control driver in a van. But don't worry, we'll be able to come home soon. Is Aunt Janice there?"

"Yeah, she's outside in the yard."

"Can you get her for me? I'll call you as often as I can and give you an update. Love you."

"Love you too Mom. I'll get Aunt Janice."

A panicked Janice, having been briefed by David, assumes the worst. I reassure her, explain what has happened and ask her to reassure David. Then I call the hospital and ask to speak to Dad's doctor. I want to make sure Dad is well enough to get the news and not have it affect his heart. The doctor decides it would be best for him to explain things to Dad, and then have him call me. I am relieved to have that burden taken from me.

Beth Murphy is the soul of efficiency and soon has me settled in yet another cozy B & B. The owner, Sadie, is obviously used to guests dealing with some type of trauma who are referred to her by hospital staff and is mother hen-like in her concern for my comfort. Beth leaves with an admonition to make sure I let her know if there is anything I need. Sadie insists on providing me a pot of tea and plate of freshly made scones and jam.

She suggests I "settle in" then come down to the "quiet room."

When I walk into the small sitting room a tray is set on a coffee table in front of a comfortable overstuffed armchair. I spend the next two hours quietly reading and drinking tea. It is restorative and I have a whole new respect for the English penchant for "a cuppa."

Rejuvenated after a ten hour sleep and buoyed by a filling English breakfast, I decide on a long walk to work the stiffness out of my bones. After lunch and a nap I choose the fifteen minute walk to the hospital over taking a cab. The hospital is bustling and I take the escalator to the third floor. Paul is sleeping so I sit in an uncomfortable chair by his bed reading the local paper I'd picked up in the hospital gift store. Nurses come and go during the next three hours, all of them assuring me my husband is "doing quite well." Such is my routine for the next four days. On day five I walk into the room and Paul is awake. I burst into tears and run to his outstretched arms, careful not to dislodge the myriad of tubing.

"Don't cry Angel. I'm fine. Sore but fine. How are you? Were you hurt?

What in the hell happened?"

I sit holding his hand and tell him as much as I know. His distress on hearing about the death of the other driver brings a nurse into the room to check his monitor. She tells him he should get some rest, meaning I've tried him out and should leave.

"I love you Angel."

I kiss him gently on the mouth.

"I love you too Paul. See you tomorrow."

Dr. Erickson is with Paul when I arrive the next afternoon.

"I've been telling your husband he's made remarkable progress and will probably be out of here day after tomorrow and able to travel three to four days after that."

"That's great. I'll start looking for flights home."

"Well, I'll leave you to your visit. By the way, how are you feeling?"

"I'm still sore and my muscles don't like being moved but I really am fine, thank you."

"Are you really fine Angel?"

"Yes. Really. More importantly, how are you?"

"I hurt like hell but I'm glad to be alive. I am looking forward to getting home."

"Me too. Paul, I'm so sorry…" I begin to cry.

"It's OK Angel. It all needed to be said. We've had a festering wound in our relationship and it's probably a good thing to finally take care of it. Once we get home we'll take a look at us and what we want for the rest of our lives together. Maybe that will mean a move, who knows. We've been given a second chance."

"I wish I had been able to talk about it a long time ago, but I didn't seem to know how. That won't be a problem from now on."

"Sounds like I could be doing a lot of listening."

We laugh, together. It's a moment of unfettered joy neither of us had felt for a long time.

"It's Tuesday. I'll see if I can get a flight home on Saturday or Sunday. Wait 'till you meet Sadie at the B & B. She's really something."

"How is David?"

"He's fine. Janice has been great. Dad's doctor told him about the accident. He called me two days ago and seemed calm enough about it. But he's adamant we are to come home and forget about finding Angelique. He thinks your accident is his fault. I told him we'll discuss it once we get home."

"We've come too far to forget it."

"We'll talk about it. I'm leaving. You get some rest. I'll see you tomorrow."

"I'm glad to have you back."

"Me too."

Before leaving England we deal with the rental car and are grateful we have adequate insurance to cover the damages. We often opt not to take the added insurance offered by the car companies. Maybe it was a sixth sense that led us to do it this time.

DALLAS, Texas

Janice, her husband Eric, David and his four cousins are all at the airport to meet us. Paul, although he looks great, is still weak and uses a cane. He'd lost almost 15 pounds. Janice packs her four in the family van while Eric drives Paul, David and me home in his car. For most of the forty minute trip we answer David's questions until he runs out of steam and decides he's heard enough.

"I'm glad to be going home. No offence Uncle Eric."

"None taken, David. There's nothing like your own place."

Once Janice has taken her family home David leaves to meet some friends and I have Paul stretch out on the couch. I automatically go into the kitchen and made a pot of tea. It's a British habit I have wholeheartedly embraced. Paul laughs when I walk into the living room with a tray of tea and biscuits.

"Nothing as soothing as a cuppa. We should call your father. Janice told me he is in the rehabilitation unit now."

"Yes. He's still pretty weak and the doctor thinks he might be developing congestive heart failure. There's the phone, bet it's him."

"Hello."

"Thank God you're home. How are you? How is Paul?"

"He's doing really well and I'm fine. I don't want you to be worried. It's not good for your heart."

"Never mind my heart. This wouldn't have happened if I had not sent you both on this crazy wild goose chase. I don't want you to do anything more about it. You get Paul well and forget an old man's fantasy. I mean it Angel. I've been filled with guilt ever since I heard about the accident."

"Dad, calm down. This wasn't your fault, not even close. It was an accident. Once Paul is strong again we'll come to Lompoc and give you the whole story about where we've been and what we've found so far. Can you wait a couple of weeks?"

"I'll wait as long as it takes. Give Paul my best. I love you Angel."

"Love you too Dad. Bye."

"Well he was in a bit of a state."

"He'll feel better when he sees you in the flesh. Now, if you'll excuse me I think I'll go have a nap on my own bed."

"I'll call you for supper."

Later that night, lying close to Paul with my arm around his waist, I realize this is where I want to be for the rest of our lives.

Life takes on a familiar hue over the next couple of weeks, as Paul grows stronger and starts checking in with his office. Because he had been so weakened by the surgery neither of us makes a move that says it's time for sex. That comes three weeks later as we are getting ready to spend a weekend with Dad. I am busy packing my suitcase and Paul is taking shirts out of the closet.

"Paul?" He turns and understands the question. He walks over, takes the suitcase off the bed and pulls me into his arms. That first explosive sex is followed by a gentler loving. We fall into a drugged sleep and wake to the phone ringing. David wants to bring a friend over for dinner. We are truly home.

Dad is watching television in the rehab centre lounge when we arrive on Saturday morning. He looks healthy and only a fine medication-induced tremor of his hands reveals anything is amiss. He hugs all of us as though we'd been lost for days in a desert. His first priority is David whom he has not seen since before his heart attack. They are very close and the affection between them always makes me smile.

"There's a cafeteria down at the end of the hallway, how about getting granddad and your folks some coffee and donuts?"

He sends David off so that we can talk about the Pink Secret. "What did you find out? Oh, if you're up to talking about it?"

We fill him in on our trekking around England and Scotland. I can see his eyes light up when we recount meeting one potential lead then dim as we are redirected elsewhere.

"So what would be a next step, if there was a next step?"

Paul and I exchange amused glances. This need to find Angelique is so acute he's brushed aside thoughts of us giving up the search. Perhaps it has something to do with the realization he might not have much time left. He knows the seriousness of congestive heart failure and is no fool when it comes to the realities of his health.

"We have a number for Katherine's brother Simon, who keeps in touch with Angelique. Katherine said she lives in Montreal but Simon wanted to alert her to the idea of possibly talking to us. Angel and I didn't want to make that call until we talked with you. You should make the decision to call him or not."

"Wow. I can't believe all you've both done. This could be it. Wow. How about you let me think about it for a few days and I'll let you know before you go home."

Dad is well enough to go out for lunch and dinner while we are there and the visit, coupled with our news, seems to put him in a buoyant mood. It is great to see him laughing, joking and telling stories. We fly home Monday night to find Dad had already left a message, the one we were expecting.

"Angel and Paul I've thought about everything and if you're both still up for it, I would be grateful if you contacted Simon. Love you all."

"I definitely knew that was coming. Your father won't rest until he sees that woman. Let's hope she's ok with stirring up the past. Remember Bridget O'Neill told us she'd been very ill in Bermuda and maybe seeing people from that period in her life is not something she wants to do."

"I suppose it's a chance we'll have to take. Like everything else on this darn quest. Let's call tomorrow."

"Hello, this is Simon. Since I'm not at home you can leave a message and I'll return your call as soon as I can. Cheers!"

"Hello Simon. This is Angeline Winterton. Your sister Katherine gave us your number and I'm calling to enquire whether you've had a chance to contact Angelique LaPierre. We appreciate your effort on our behalf. Hope to talk to you soon. Bye."

"You didn't leave our number."

I call back and leave the number. My nervousness at not leaving the number had sent my heart rate up.

"Well, now we wait for Simon."

We waited and waited. And waited. Dad would call periodically and not ask what he really wanted to know. Our answer was always the same.

"No call."

David and I return to our respective workplaces and begin talking about our future in Texas, or not. Two months later Dad is ready to leave rehab and return to his own home. He seems to have escaped the congestive heart failure diagnosis, at least for now. We all fly back to Lompoc to help him settle in. He is happier than I'd seen him since before his attack. Even though he is feeling great he is sensible enough to agree to have a nurse check in with him several times a week.

He doesn't mention Angelique. Neither do we.

Several days later I come home from work having stopped at the grocery store. David is on the phone and waving frantically. I'm afraid something has happened to Dad.

"Some guy with an accent wants to talk to you."

"Hello. It's Angeline."

"This is Simon Alderton. How are you?"

"Oh, fine. Just fine. And you?"

"Wonderful. Thank you. Now, I understand you want to talk with Angelique."

"Yes."

"Well, I've had a word with her and she was intrigued that you want to speak with her."

I wait.

"She's thought it over and I'm afraid…"

My heart sank.

"…I'm afraid she's going to be out of the country for three weeks starting tomorrow, but she would be pleased to talk with you when she returns."

"That's wonderful. Thank you so much. I can't tell you how much I appreciate this."

"Here's the number…"

I write it down with shaking fingers.

"It's a Montreal number."

"Thank you again Simon."

"Yes, well. Good luck with it. Cheerio."

"Bye."

I stare at the number on the paper in my clenched fingers.

"I can't believe it. I just can't believe it."

Not waiting for Paul to come home, I call to tell him the news. We're both as giddy as teenagers. We also both agree that we won't tell Dad until we've spoken with Angelique.

"It's going to seem like a long three weeks."

It is difficult to not tell Dad we are going to be talking to Angelique. But if she decides not to talk to us, for one reason or another, it will be too great a disappointment for him. As tempting as it is to blurt it out during our many conversations, I manage to keep it to myself.

Paul and I talk about what we want to ask Angelique and wonder how we are to get around to the big question – would she travel to California to visit Dad since he would not be allowed to fly because of his heart. We start working on a list of questions to be ready for the phone call. It makes us feel like we are still engaged in the quest. We decide to give her several days to get unpacked and settled. It's also a bit of a delaying tactic. On Tuesday evening I dial Angelique's number.

"Hello. This is Angelique. Bonjour."

"Hi. My name is Angeline. I'm Mark Forrester's daughter. I believe you knew each other in Bermuda. Simon Alderton gave me your number."

"Yes. Simon did tell me you might be calling. I must say this is quite a surprise. How is your father?"

"That's actually the reason for this call and why we've been trying to find you."

"I'm intrigued. Is this something you want to do on the phone or would you like to come to visit here? That certainly would be my preference. And you are most welcome to stay with us while you're in Montreal."

I ask Angelique to hold and check with Paul. He agrees we should visit.

"My husband Paul and I would also prefer to talk with you in person. When would it be convenient for us to come to Montreal?"

"Next weekend would work for us. We have no plans, if that works for you."

"Yes. That would be great. Would Saturday afternoon around 2 be convenient?"

"Absolutely. Our address is 110 Cote St. Antoine in Westmount. And you have our phone number."

"Thank you Angelique. We'll see you next weekend."

"I look forward to it. Bye"

"Wow. Wow. I cannot believe I have actually spoken with the elusive Angelique. It seems surreal after all we've been through."

"And to think she's right here on this continent."

"Yeah. Go figure. I need a glass of wine."

"We should tell your father." He hands me the phone.

Needless to say Dad is overwhelmed by the news. I quickly remind him not to get his hopes up in case she does not want to travel to California.

"She'll come. I just know she will. You'll see."

"Ok Dad. I just don't want you to be too disappointed if it doesn't work out."

"Don't worry Angel. It will work out. You and Paul have done the hard work. It will work out fine."

"OK Dad. We'll call when we get back from Montreal."

"Well Dad is on cloud nine. I sure hope he's not getting himself worked up for a big letdown. Realistically, this woman is being asked to travel across the continent to see a man she knew when she was a kid. He's a stranger now. She's probably married with a family. What are they going to think?"

"I guess we'll find out next weekend. I have to tell you I'll be glad when this quest is completed and our lives go back to being a little less exciting."

"I don't disagree Paul. But while it's been trying and difficult in some ways, in others it's been a blessing. Especially for the two of us."

"That's true and for that I am truly grateful. I'm even grateful for the accident. What's a liver when the future of your marriage is at stake." He laughs and pulls me into his arms.

"In future we should try simpler ways of getting each other's attention."

"Let's get into something more comfortable and discuss it as soon as we've had dinner."

"Agreed. Let's get cooking."

On Saturday morning we board an American Airlines flight in Dallas, change flights in Detroit and head to Montreal. I'd always wanted to visit but never thought it would be to track down Dad's old girlfriend. Even though Paul and I have been immersed in this venture for months I still often shake my head when the incongruity of it hits me. There are those who would definitely consider me certifiable. I almost consider me certifiable.

MONTREAL

At noon we are checking into the Queen Elizabeth hotel. We decide to do some sightseeing and eat in a French bistro, some place we might not find in Dallas.

The concierge is full of advice and from him we learn the address we'll be visiting is a twenty minute cab ride. He arranges for us to be picked up at 1:30 to ensure on-time arrival. I don't think I'm nervous until Paul gently pulls my right thumb out of my teeth. There's not much of the nail left.

Paul hands the driver two twenties and gets little in change. He adds five and hands it back. We get out of the cab and stand staring at the house. I'm willing myself back in Dallas. The two-storey brick house has large picture windows on either side of a big oak door. It sits in what looks like several acres of forest and there appears to be a mile of flower beds.

"Pretty nice place."

"Yep."

"Want to go up and knock?"

"I guess. Since we're here." My inane attempt at levity.

We walk up the driveway lined with a sea of colourful flowers and shrubs. I push my heart out of my throat. This is it.

Paul pushes the bell. We hear it ring then footsteps inside. I'm not sure what to expect. I'd only seen photos of Angelique when she was a teenager and a few theatre photos.

The door opens and she's standing in front of us. In a flash I take in the green shift dress and gold cardigan, the pearls, bare legs, black low heel pumps and blond hair in a ponytail. She's at least sixty-five years old and has a ponytail. She welcomes us with her whole body from her laughing eyes to her hearty handshake that seems to involve her entire torso.

"Hi, I'm Angelique. Welcome to Montreal."

We introduce ourselves and are taken into the library. And it is a true library. Every inch of every wall space has a bookcase. The soft, well-worn brown leather easy chairs make you want to stay and put your feet up. She says she's made tea and brings in a large tray of tea and an assortment of home-made cookies.

"This must be very important for you to come all this way to see me."

"I am sure it must seem very strange to you…"

"I stopped being surprised by unusual situations a very long time ago. So tell me what it is you need from me."

"My father has had a very serious heart attack and even before he was allowed to leave the hospital he asked if Paul and I would find you. He believes he is going to die soon and wants to see you one last time. Needless to say I hope he does not die soon but I love him very much and want to do what I can to grant his wish."

"What does your mother think of this unusual request?"

"Mom died many years ago."

"I'm terribly sorry. I know how devastating it is to lose your mother. You never stop missing her."

"No. I still grieve for her. Somehow, I don't think she'd mind that Dad wants to see you before he dies."

"What makes you say that?"

I tell her about the conversation I had with mom on her death bed.

"Your mother was an extraordinary woman. And a generous one. Your father was a lucky man. I am truly touched he has had such fond memories of me all these years. My goodness, I was just a teenager and he was so much more mature. All I could think of was moving on. I felt very badly about leaving when he asked me to stay. He was a wonderful man and if I had been older things might have been different for us. Is he well enough to travel?"

"His doctor has advised against it. But I know if coming here to Montreal is the only hope he has to see you he will defy the doctor and do it. I think the thought of possibly finding you kept him alive during the first days after his attack."

"I must say I am somewhat stunned by this. He is remembering a young girl but the woman is now sixty-five. Your father is eight years older than me. It's interesting how it's an age difference that doesn't seem as significant as it did when I was nineteen. I made a big deal of that age difference."

"I really don't think he thinks about that. As Angeline has indicated you left a lasting impression on his heart and it's a part of him that's never gotten over you. I know it's a terrible imposition but would you be willing to come to California to see him? He would pay for your expenses."

"I wouldn't be concerned about the expenses. But I do have to discuss all of this with my husband. I must say my friendship with your father is not something that's ever come up in our conversations."

"Oh, of course. I'm sorry. We've been talking about this just thinking about ourselves."

"Angeline and I don't want to impose any more than we have to nor make things awkward for you."

"Don't worry, you're not imposing and my husband is a rather wonderful man who will find this amusing and consider it a compliment to me."

"He sounds like an unusual guy."

"He is, Paul. Now, would you like to come back for dinner? I know he will want to meet you both. Our granddaughter is staying with us for a few days and I'm certain she will find this all very dramatic."

"Thank you. But we really don't want to impose."

"One thing you'll learn about me is that I don't issue an invitation unless I really want to and unless I know my husband will appreciate it. Life is too short to waste time pretending."

"Then thank you again, we'd love to. What time would you like us here?"

"How about seven? That way we can eat by eight. We tend to be late eaters – will that be Ok with you both?"

"Absolutely. Angeline and I want to tour around Montreal so we'll go back to the hotel and take one of their scheduled tours of the city."

"Enjoy yourselves. It's a beautiful city. Make sure you go to Old Montreal."

"We will. Would you mind if we call a cab? We have the number here."

"Of course not." She hands Paul the phone.

The cab will take ten minutes. We talk about living in Dallas and David. She asks about Bridget O'Neill and we talk about our visit to Bermuda until the cab arrives.

"Well, I'll look forward to seeing you both later." We shake hands.

As we walk through the door I feel compelled to turn around. I take Angelique's hand again.

"I can't thank you enough for seeing us. Whatever you decide I really appreciate your understanding."

"It's my pleasure. See you later."

Driving away from Angelique's home Paul and I are silent for several blocks.

"WOW!"

"Yeah, WOW!"

"She's sixty-five going on forty. She hasn't changed much from her photo."

"A few more crinkles around the eyes but, holy crap, Paul."

"I don't know if seeing her when he can't have her is going to be enough for your father once he gets a look at her, even now."

"It will have to be. She seems to have a pretty solid marriage."

"Lucky guy."

"We'll get to meet him in person in, oh, about four hours. He must be something if she's crazy about him."

"She'll find your dad is still in pretty good shape. Except for his bad heart. He was a pretty handsome dude in that blue uniform. Most women would not have walked away that easily."

"I don't think it was that easy. She seemed to care for Dad."

"Just didn't love him enough."

"I guess it just wasn't meant to be."

"Guess not."

We take the 3:30 p.m. bus tour from the hotel and spend almost two hours enjoying a tour of new and old Montreal. Back at the hotel we decide to stroll into the downtown, find a bistro, sit outside and people watch. We are both excited and anxious about the evening so a glass of wine and friendly banter with our table neighbours was just what we needed to ease the tension.

Angelique and Jon are also sharing a glass of wine and Jon listens intently to the unusual story and request involving his beloved wife. She is a balm to his soul and his heart lurches in his chest several times as the story unfolds. But by the end he is intrigued by the man who has loved his Angelique through a lifetime.

"That's quite a story. Are you going to visit this Mark?"

"I'm not sure Jon. What do you think? How would you feel about me going to visit him? It's a pretty strange situation."

"If you mean would I be jealous? Only a bit, and not enough to ask you not to go."

"Really?"

"This is obviously a man you cared about, maybe even loved at the time, and I know you're feeling badly for him. And, I know in your heart you think it would be the right thing to do to grant his wish to see you one last time. And, I fully understand why he would want to see you."

"Kiss me. It's the best way to keep you quiet."

He laughs and does.

Deciding what to wear to dinner is difficult. I don't want to over or under dress and instinctively know Angelique will be perfectly dressed. I decide on a white shift dress with a red enamel necklace, paired with a red belt, black shoes and handbag. Paul approved, so much so I had to push him away to get into his black pants, blue shirt and light grey jacket.

"We'll do," he announces, looking at us in the mirror.

"We'll have to. We have to go. It's 6:30."

Exactly at 7 p.m. we ring Angelique's doorbell for the second time that day.

Footsteps. This time heavier.

The door opens and a tall, good looking man with grey curly hair, wearing grey pants and a navy blazer greets us with the friendliness we saw in Angelique.

"Angeline and Paul. Welcome. I'm Jon Buchan. Please, come in."

He takes us into the living room and within minutes Angelique comes in to greet us. She hugs us and it seems perfectly natural. We sit and Jon asks what we would like to drink, offering Paul a choice of several beers. Angelique and I opt for red wine. They have a lovely South African Jon says I would probably like. I do.

For the next hour we have a fascinating conversation on a myriad of topics from the politics of the U.S. and Canada and our friendly relations to world conflict, gardening and the latest Hollywood blockbuster. Both Angelique and Jon leave the room to check on dinner preparations at various times, never leaving us alone.

Just after 8 p.m. the door opens and in comes a clone of Angelique. She greets her grandparents in a way that tells an onlooker they are dearly loved. We learn she calls them G-mere and G-pere, her way of shortening the French words for grandmother and grandfather, grand-mere and grand-pere. She turns her attention to us.

"Hello, you must be Angeline and Paul. I'm Roni. Pleased to meet you both."

She shakes hands with the fervour of her grandmother.

"Nice to meet you too, Roni." Paul and I are mesmerized by this charming teenager who causes the room to light up.

"Our granddaughter is sixteen and loves to talk."

"You're unbelievably like your grandmother."

"Oh, yeah, that's another thing they have in common," Jon says teasing his wife.

"Glad you made it in time for dinner sweetie. Now, if you would all like to make your way into the dining room."

Jon leads us down a short hallway, pass the library where we had tea earlier in the day, and into the dining room which is open to the kitchen. Elegant and simple, warm and friendly. Those words describe everything about this household and the people in it.

Roni, announcing she intends to become a photojournalist, picks up the camera bag she has deposited near the front door and begins taking photos.

"I like to document things, so I'm documenting your visit. I'll email you the photos."

Jon shakes his head in amusement.

"Do you mind? I promise you she won't be unobtrusive or discreet."

We all laugh. She shoots a dozen photos and then sits at the table.

We pass around the large bowls of boeuf bourguignon, green beans and boiled potatoes. Jon pours wine for everyone.

"To new friends."

We all toast to new friends.

The dinner conversation initially revolves around Roni and her various activities during the day. She asks us a hundred questions and in short order knows everything about us, including details about David. She can't seem to hear enough about Texas and everything American.

"I didn't think young people in Canada particularly liked Americans or our way of life."

"We don't all feel that way, only the closed minded. But, they're entitled to their opinion. I just don't share it. I love the U.S. I'd live there in a heartbeat."

"I don't know if the young guys in the States would be ready for you."

Paul's quip makes her laugh, a musical laugh that tempts one to tell her funny things just to hear it. She also has the good manners to know when she has exceeded her time holding forth and concentrates on her food.

Eventually the conversation turns to the topic of our visit. It is evident that Angelique and Jon have had a thorough discussion about our unorthodox request. It is also quite evident that Jon adores his Angelique and she him. It is an enviable relationship and one I vow to develop with Paul.

"It seems your father had very good taste in women. From what Angelique tells me your mother was a wonderful person, and my Angelique is a pretty special woman."

"Yes. My mom was great. You must find this a very weird situation?"

"I must say at first it sounded pretty crazy but Angelique has that effect on people, especially on guys."

"Jon. Stop it."

Their eyes meet with laughter. My heart lurches. Angelique smiles at me and looks at Paul.

"I know you must be on tenterhooks wanting to know what we've decided."

I laugh nervously.

"I have to admit…"

"Well Jon and I have decided I should go visit your father."

"You have? Thank you. Are you sure Angelique?"

"Yes, we're sure. As a matter of fact it will work out well for us because Jon will be in Los Angeles next month to promote his new book."

"What kind of novels do you write?"

"Political junk. People seem to like it."

"My husband is being modest. His last two books have been bestsellers in Canada. I will fly to Lompoc on Thursday the 16th and Jon will go to LA, then he'll come to Lompoc on Monday so that we can fly home together on Wednesday. Would that work for you and your father?"

"Yes. Absolutely it would. Dad will be so happy. You are both very special people to be doing this for us. Especially you Jon. Thank you for your understanding. I'm not so sure many men would feel comfortable about something like this."

Jon looks across at Angelique.

"If everything we mean to each other could be undone by Angelique visiting a dear friend from her past we would be on shaky ground. I hope seeing Angelique one more time will help ease that ache inside him. And I'm looking forward to meeting him myself, even though he may hate me."

We all laugh, except Roni.

"Will someone please tell me what this conversation is about? Or is it none of my business? Please don't tell me it's not my business. It sounds far too juicy and I'll go insane wanting to know."

She looks at each of us. Waiting.

We let her wait. Jon takes pity on her.

"It really isn't any of your business, but...your G-mere had a good friend when she lived in Bermuda who turns out to be Angeline's father..."

Before he can continue Roni jumps in.

" G-mere, was he your 'flyboy?' Oh. Oh. He was wasn't he? Oh, this is amazing."

"And how do you know about G-mere's flyboy as you call him?"

"The night of her party G-mere told me there was this nice man in Bermuda who helped her when she was really sick. He was the only person besides her roommates she would let see her deformed face. Ah, sorry G-mere."

"That's OK Roni. It was deformed. And yes, Mark was my flyboy."

"Would you like me to continue?" Jon asks, laughing at his granddaughter.

"Sorry G-pere. Go on."

"Angeline's father wants to see your G-mere. He has had a serious heart attack and is worried he won't see her again before he dies. It appears he loved your G-mere very much."

"I can see that. She's loveable. Look at you, you're besotted with her."

"You can see our granddaughter has a lot of cheek for a sixteen year old and often makes grand statements of exaggeration, but in this case she is right on the money."

We all laugh again. The whole evening is filled with laughter.

"So?" Roni aims her question at her grandmother.

"So?"

"So, are you going? For real?"

"Yes. I'm going for real."

She turns her steely green eyes on her grandfather.

"And you're really going to meet the flyboy?"

"I am."

"Oh boy. I have to be there too. Can I come?"

"Does your cheekiness know no bounds?"

"Ah, G-mere, you can't leave me out of this. I'd love to meet flyboy too."

"Roni, careful, you're talking about the father of our guest."

"Sorry G-pere. Sorry Angeline. Angeline. That's almost like Angelique. Was that, did your father, ah, did you…"

"Well, well. Now there's a rarity. Our granddaughter is at a loss for words. Probably from the embarrassment caused by her inappropriate question. Our apologies Angeline."

"No. No. Please, it's OK. It's pretty smart of her to pick up on the similarity of our names. Now that you've brought it up, Paul and I also wondered about it so I asked my mother before she died. It appears that she loved my father so much she gave me a name that was as close to Angelique as she could without my father being aware of what she was doing. She never told him and I've never asked him about it."

"Are you going to ask him before he dies?"

"Roni!" her grandparents say in unison.

"It's OK. I'm not sure Roni. Right now I cannot think about my father dying. It's much too painful. But if your grandparents would like to bring you to California with them, we would be delighted."

"Thank you so much. That's fab. Hear that? I can come with you. Is it OK?"

"We'll see. Your G-mere will talk to your parents. So don't nag us every day."

"Promise."

Angelique and Jon exchanged knowing, amused glances.

"Now that we've settled the biggest question of the evening, let's go into the library while Roni makes some tea, or would you both prefer coffee?"

We settle on tea.

Another thirty minutes pass quickly, mainly because of the ease of conversation with our hosts. However, the emotion of the evening has also been physically taxing. I make a futile attempt to stifle a yawn. It is not lost on Angelique.

"Look at us, we're enjoying your company so much we're not paying attention to the time. You must be exhausted. Roni, would you mind running Angeline and Paul back to the QE?"

"I'd be glad to."

"That's very kind. We could get a cab."

"Absolutely not. I am happy to do it."

We are warmly hugged by our hosts and agree to talk on the phone in a couple of weeks to finalize details of their visit. Despite my fatigue it is difficult to leave the warmth of that friendly home.

Roni's lively conversation keeps us awake during the drive to the hotel and she offers to take us to one of her favourite places, St. Joseph's Oratory, the following morning. She insists and we accept. She pulls up in front of the hotel and gets out, giving us hugs that are like vice grips, promising to be back at 10 a.m. She drives away honking the horn and waving her arm out the window.

We find it difficult to sleep and spend the next two hours reviewing the tapes of the evening.

"That Jon's quite the guy. He is sure taking this bizarre situation amazingly well. He really does seem to see it as a great compliment to his wife. I wonder how your father is going to deal with it all."

"I have a feeling Dad will be so grateful to see Angelique he won't even mind meeting her husband."

"I keep trying to get my head around his obsession with her. It's been over forty years. Forty. And a lot of water under the bridge. Maybe he wants to see if she got old and fat without him."

"Oh you." I swat him with my pillow. He grabs my arm and pulls me to his chest. His hands begin a skilled exploration that leaves a trail of heat on a body he knows so well. Angelique and my father are soon forgotten.

Roni is as good as her word and pulls up in front of the hotel exactly at 10 a.m.

"Hi Angeline. Hi Paul. Oh sorry. Mother told me to ask for permission to call you by your first names. She and Dad are sticklers. I could call you Mr. and Mrs. Winterton, If you prefer."

Her old fashioned manners are charming. We both tell her to call us by our first names. I think that was a first for us. At the Oratory we stand in line with several dozen other tourists to take the official tour and Roni's camera got a workout.

By the time it is over we are all hungry and Roni suggests several restaurant choices in the area. We opt for La Petite Creperie where, she assures us, we will find the world's best and biggest selection of crepes, with wonderful wine to compliment them. She is right on both counts. During lunch she keeps us entertained with stories about her childhood, growing up in Montreal and several other Canadian cities, her love for all things American and her quite conservative views on how the world should be run. Talkative, but self aware for a young teenager, she apologizes many times for her tendency to "blabber on," then asks questions, paying rapt attention to the answers, mostly without interruption until the end of a story or explanation. The two hour lunch ends too soon.

Her upbringing prompts her to ask if there is anywhere else we would like to go. While we would have enjoyed her delightful company for the rest of the day, I sense she has places to be. Thanking her, I explain we had window shopped in the hotel and saw three or four boutiques we want to visit.

"If you're absolutely sure."

"We are."

The hugs she gave us this time were heartfelt and, we both later agreed, held a tinge of sadness we were leaving Montreal the next day. But then a memory from the evening before brings back her effervescence.

"Oh. That's right. I'm probably coming to visit you with G-mere and

G-pere. Excellent. Enjoy the rest of your visit. Thanks for coming with me today."

"The pleasure was all ours Roni. Angeline and I can't thank you and your grandparents enough for your kindness and hospitality. You've all treated us like family."

"Well, you are, sort of, in a way. Well, bye. I'll send you lots of photos."

She ducks back into the driver's seat, waves excitedly and drives off.

It would have been great to stay in Montreal for another week but we are anxious to get home to Texas and fly to Lompoc to see Dad. We decide it would be best to tell him everything in person.

DALLAS

David is waiting at the airport and fills us in on the goings on in the city and the latest calamities to befall Janice's brood. Fortunately, it's nothing that has permanently maimed any of them. Their lives are a constant round of sprains, bruises, pranks, surprises and oddities fiction couldn't rival.

Getting home takes almost an hour and we are able to fill David in on our visit. More of a listener than a talker, he absorbs everything, asking questions only when he needs more detail. I can't help but think of the contrast between the young chatterbox we'd left in Montreal and our more introspective son. It crosses my mind they might be meeting in a couple of months. Now, won't that be interesting.

We had hoped to spend a week getting reorganized before flying to Lompoc but Dad is so anxious to hear about Angelique we decide to fly out in two days. We heed David's piteous urgings not to be sent back to Janice's and take him with us.

LOMPOC

Dad greets us at the door with the energy of a young buck. If I didn't know personally how serious his heart condition is I would say he was in the best of health. Paul and I find it quite amusing. His hug is certainly not that of a fragile seventy-three year old.

"Come on in."

I have to give Dad credit. He tries very hard to hold back the questions we know he is so anxious to ask. He waits until we are sitting at the dinner table.

"Well, how is she? Does she remember me? Does she think I'm insane for asking you to track her down?"

"Yes, Dad, she does remember you and no, she doesn't think you're insane. She actually found it rather touching that you want to see her. She did agree it was rather unusual for a daughter to be tracking down her father's old girlfriend. And I can see why you wanted to find her. She's quite something."

Mark takes a worn photo from his wallet. He looks at for a few seconds then hands it to Paul.

"Would you recognize her from this?"

"What you mean is does she still look like that." We all laugh at Dad's transparency.

"Actually, she does. You would certainly have no trouble recognizing her and you'll get to judge for yourself. She's agreed to come to see you."

For a moment I thought I would be the cause of my father having a stroke. The wineglass is frozen halfway to his lips and the blood drains from his face.

"Dad. Oh God, Dad! Say something. Paul, take the glass from him."
As I rush to his side he lets out the breath he's been holding.

"I'm OK Angel. Sit down please. I was just momentarily shocked by
the words I was hearing. I wanted to hear them so badly I was preparing
myself for the opposite. Did she really agree to come out here?"

"Yes, she did. And what's more, her husband is coming with her."

"And their granddaughter, Roni, with an 'i.'"

"Their granddaughter?" We all look at David.

"Yes, she's about your age. A year or so older."

"Does she look like her grandmother?" He asks, trying to be casual
about it.

"Spitting image," Paul tells him. "And a similar personality."

"Why is her husband coming with her?" I can tell Dad has been trying
to digest that bit of the information.

"He is going to be in Los Angeles for a book launch the week of the 13th
of next month. Angelique and Roni will come to Lompoc on Thursday
the 16th and Jon will join them the following Monday. They plan to
fly back to Montreal on Wednesday. You'll like him Dad. Paul and I
got along with them both, which isn't difficult because they're lovely
people."

"Roni with an 'I,' what's that short for?"

We all turn to look at David.

"Just wondering."

We all take turns teasing him until he threatens to leave the table if we
don't stop. We apologize and Paul takes pity on his son.

"I don't know son. It might be her actual name."

"Are we coming to Lompoc when they're here?"

"Yes," Paul and I say in unison. We all laugh.

After dinner Dad announces he's going for his evening walk. David hits the books and Paul decides to watch one of his favourite crime shows on TV. Something tells me to accompany Dad.

"Want some company on that walk?"

"If you're offering, I'm accepting."

We pull on light jackets and head down Palmetto Avenue. Even as a young girl I was fascinated by the tall Palmetto palms lining the avenue that seemed to almost reach the sky. I've often marvelled at the joy and uniqueness of having lived in one house in one neighbourhood my entire childhood and now being able to bring my own child here.

I tuck my arm in Dad's and he gives me a side hug.

"You're a great daughter. Have I told you that?"

"On several occasions," I tell him, laughing. "I never get tired of hearing it. But I am what you helped make me. You and Mom."

"I sometimes feel so disloyal to your mother because of my obsession with Angelique. Yet, I really don't mean to be. I loved your mother very much. We were great friends and shared a good life together. I only hope I made her as happy as she made me all those years."

"Mom knew you loved her. She never doubted it for a moment." I hesitate. Then before my mind could stop my lips the next words came tumbling out.

"She knew about Angelique."

"We had a lot in common, your mother an…what did you say?"

"Here, let's sit over here in the park."

It's the second shock I've landed on him tonight and one could wonder if I am trying to off the poor man.

"No. She didn't. She couldn't possibly have known. Angelique has never come up between us. It's just not possible. She would have let it slip, somehow."

I told him everything Mom had told me during our last conversation.

"So, you see Dad, even down to giving me a name similar to Angelique's, Mom not only knew but understood what was in your heart. But she also knew it did not diminish the love you felt for her and she never felt betrayed."

I had been staring out at the street and when I turn towards him I see tears slowly rolling down my dad's aging cheek. It damn near breaks my heart. I hand him a tissue.

The lump in my throat is the size of a melon and I can't speak, even if I want to. I know enough to let Dad weep. He is weeping for the wife he loved and for her generosity in allowing him to have loved another woman. The complications of life make me want to scream. For a moment I want everything to disappear. I want to be six again, before I knew about the Pink Project, before, before, before.

As if sensing my pain, Dad gets himself under control and puts his arm around my shoulders, drawing me close. I rest my head against his arm, wanting to feel the comfort a child needs and seeks from a parent. For a moment I'm tempted to tell him I also knew about the pink hat but somehow, as my grief subsides somewhat, an inner voice tells me to hold my tongue. His next words make me glad I did.

"I can only be grateful this was something that didn't affect your life Angel. That would compound the guilt I feel that your mother knew about Angelique all those years and never said anything. Not only that, she loved me enough to actually understand my obsession. I have not been worthy of her and it breaks my heart."

"Dad, please, there is absolutely no reason you should feel like this. It wasn't an issue for Mom. She knew you loved her. Angelique was special to you and sometimes those kinds of relationships live in our hearts forever. You can't pretend it never happened. Mom understood and she was good with it. But that was because she also knew and believed you loved her. She would not want you to be feeling guilty. And I don't. We had a wonderful life and you are a great father. If that wasn't the case I would not have trekked across the globe trying to find Angelique."

"I shouldn't have been so selfish. I'm sorry."

"Dad, I've told you before there is no need to be sorry about anything. Paul and I did it because we wanted to. And it paid off, we found her. Now she's going to come to see you. Come on, let's go back. I could use a cup of tea."

"Tea?"

"Yeah. It's my new British addiction. I drink pots of it."

On the walk back to the house Dad and I talk about David, his cardiac exercise problem and the grim state of the U.S. economy. Anything but Angelique. At home as I'm plugging in the kettle Dad tells me he's going to bed, gives me a hug and says "I've decided I'm not going to invite Angelique here. I know you and Paul won't be happy about it but I can't do it. I can't betray your mother. And, I don't really want to talk about it right now Angel. But I've made up my mind. Good night. I'll see you in the morning."

"What are you saying, Dad? This is crazy. You've wanted this all your life. All you're going to do is see her and talk. How is that betraying Mom?"

"There's no use talking about it Angel."

He leaves and I stand in the kitchen stunned by his announcement. I turn off the kettle and go to our room to talk to Paul. I nudge him awake.

"Paul, we have a problem. Dad's on a guilt trip and doesn't want Angelique to come to visit. We have to do something. I've told him he's got nothing to be guilty about but he's not listening. God. Me and my big mouth. I feel terrible having to tell Angelique after the two of us trekking across the world to find her he's decided to be loyal to Mom's memory and doesn't want to see her now. I can't stand the idea of having to phone her and tell her. He's not being logical. We have to do something."

"I got that. What happened? "

"I told him Mom knew about Angelique and the pink hat."

"Why?"

"It just came tumbling out. I couldn't stop my lips. It just seemed like the right thing to do at that moment."

"Wow. OK. Well, do you have anything in mind?"

"I'm too upset to figure anything out. I was hoping you might come up with something."

"Maybe we should give him some time to think about it. He's probably just feeling a bit disloyal to your mother because he knows he's going to be seeing Angelique. There is no way he'll refuse to see her at this point. Do you want me to talk to him?"

"Would you? We can't give him too long because Angelique will be booking her flights. I'll go for a run in the morning so you can talk to him over breakfast."

"Oh good. He won't suspect a thing, especially since you've not been running for the past two years."

"I'll just say I need to get in shape and I'm starting to run again. I don't really care if he does suspect I've left you alone to talk to him. He has to see reason."

"Why?

"Because it's something he's wanted all his life and I know he really still does, no matter what he's saying."

"He's a grown man. He's allowed to change his mind."

"But I've told you I know he doesn't want to. But he may be hard to convince to change his mind. He sure seemed adamant about it."

"Well, I'll try, but don't get your hopes up."

"Thanks Paul. I've got to get some sleep. I'm totalled."

"And you have a long run in the morning. Ah, you're groaning now but just wait 'till you take to the sidewalk Aren't you going to take your clothes off."

"No! Good night. Don't say anything else. I'm too stressed. Goodnight."

In the morning I am tempted to hide out and listen to the conversation between Dad and Paul but thinking better of it, I leave the house before they are up. While I have no intention of running, I knew it was going to be a very long walk. I console myself with the thought that since I had been gone a long time this would give me a chance to visit streets and places I knew so well as a child but have not seen in 2twenty years. I decide not to dwell on what might be happening back at the house.

When Paul rolls over to see Angeline's place empty his thoughts soon turn to the task ahead. He is not looking forward to it. Angeline wants him to convince her father and he's not so sure he can, or that he should. Walking into the kitchen he is drawn to the smell coming from the coffee pot. Mark is already up and reading the paper.

"Angel sleeping in?"

"No. No. She went for a run. She's on a fit kick again."

"Really?"

"Yeah." Mark thinks "Oh great, he suspects something fishy is going on."

124

He didn't have long to wait.

"I imagine her ploy is to have you persuade me to invite Angelique here for a visit? I've known my daughter a long time."

"Sorry. She was getting too emotional about it. I must admit Mark, I don't quite understand why you've changed your mind about seeing her."

"When Angel told me her mother knew about Angelique I felt ashamed. It was like a betrayal of her loyalty. Imagine loving someone that much. I feel so damn guilty about my feelings for Angelique. If I ask her to come here it will be the final insult to that unconditional love Margie had for me."

"Do you hear what you're saying Mark? Margie loved you unconditionally. She understood the place Angelique had in your heart but she never felt threatened because you never gave her a reason to doubt your love for her. I can't imagine she would want you to refuse to see Angelique."

"I don't know Paul. It just doesn't seem right."

"Think about it. All you're doing is asking her to come to California to visit. She's an old friend. And she's married. And wants to stay that way. Look, just think about it. But you should make a final decision by tomorrow because Angelique and Jon will be making their reservations in a day or two."

"I will. Thanks Mark. Now, I'm off to the cardiac centre. An hour of cardio and weights to keep me above ground a little longer. Here's Angel. Follow my lead. How was your run?"

"Great. I'm a bit out of shape."

"A few weeks and you'll be back in the groove."

"Yeah. So, did you guys have a good chat?"

"We always do. I'm off. I'll be back for lunch. Let's go to the Organic Leaf. They have a few items on the menu I can eat that's good for my heart and I actually like. See you both later."

I watch as Dad jaunts out of the kitchen and see him walk past the window with a spring in his step.

"So?"

"So?"

"What did you talk about?'

"This and that. Exercise."

"Paul don't be aggravating, you know what I mean. Did you talk to him about Angelique?"

"Yes."

" Don't be aggravating. Tell me what Dad said." I follow him into the living room. "Is he going to ask her to come to see him? What did he say exactly?"

"He'll think about it."

"You know you can be very aggravating. What's your gut feeling?"

"I think he'll ask her to come. I suggested it be soon."

"Great. I'm starving. Let's have breakfast. Wake David."

By the time we finish doing a few chores around the house and in the garden Dad is back and we all go to lunch. Dad can tell I am champing at the bit but he isn't giving me a hint. I decide to preserve my sanity and stop worrying about it. I am going to have to wait until he is ready and that's the end of it.

Driving us to the airport the next afternoon Dad is relaxed and happy. He shakes hands with Paul, leans in to his ear and appears to tell him something.

He gives me his usual warm, loving hug but doesn't lean in to my ear. I

126

feel a bit peeved. Once we are settled in our seats I ask Paul what Dad had whispered.

"I thought you'd never ask. What took you so long?"

"Don't start that again. Just tell me."

"He said to tell you he decided to put you out of your misery and asked me to tell you..."

The air attendant begins her take off instructions.

"What? What?"

"He's going to invite her."

"Thank God. When?" I say rather loudly and people turn to stare. I get quiet.

"He called her before we had lunch yesterday."

Paul hands me a newspaper and I'm not sure I read a word of it, at least not one that registers in my brain. Angelique is not only part of Dad's past she is strangely a part of mine and I tell myself, not without a tinge of guilt myself, Mom would understand.

MONTREAL

Angelique slowly hangs up the phone and walks in to the library. Jon looks up from his newspaper.

"Would I be correct in guessing that was your flyboy from California?"

"It was my flyboy as you and our granddaughter keep calling him."

"It was what you called him."

"That's different. Anyway, he has invited me to California for a visit. Even offered to pay for the trip and my hotel, but I thanked him kindly and said I would take care of my own expenses."

"Are you doing this just because he might be on borrowed time or do you really want to go? You don't have any obligation to fly off to California just because an old love from your past wants you to."

"I know that. Yes, I would like to go. He was a lovely man and I guess I do feel that this is something I should do. It appears I caused him some grief when I was a teenager and I really would like to do this. I feel it's the least I can do. Does that make sense?"

"From you sweetheart it makes perfect sense. Are we going to stick to the travel plans we discussed with Flyboy's, sorry, Mark's daughter and son-in-law?" His tone of voice surprises Angelique and she wonders if Jon is just a bit jealous, but she doesn't comment on it.

"Yes, I think so. Mark said that also works for him. I thought maybe Roni could fly down and meet us in Lompoc once you get there. We can always extend our stay, rent a car and spend another week sightseeing along the California coast. He said he is looking forward to meeting you."

"I just bet."

"Jon!"

Getting out of his chair he comes over to where I'm standing near the fireplace and puts his arms around me.

"Sweetheart, I put myself in his place and I know if you were coming to see me under these circumstances, and having an unrequited love for you all my life, the last person I'd want to see is your husband. But, I will be happy to meet this man. In fact, I can hardly wait. My curiosity has been in overdrive ever since Angeline and Mark were here."

"So, you have an ulterior motive?"

"You bet. I'll be watching him like a hawk. Sweetheart, don't look so horrified. I'm joking. Kind of…now kiss me."

"You're a remarkable man. Have I told you that?"

"Only the thousand times, but I can hear it again. Want lunch made by me or Helene at the Bistro Pub?"

"Let's go see Helene." He laughs again as I get my purse. The joy of him makes me forget the phone call from Mark and it's only as I walk up the stairs the sound of Mark's voice comes back to me. I actually recognized the timbre of it after all those years and he sounded like the man I knew when he was only 27. There was a tug in my heart when he told me with such sincerity how wonderful it was to hear my voice. This was going to be an interesting visit.

LOMPOC

Mark stands in front of the mirror in his bathroom adjusting his tie for the tenth time. His aging hands tremble. He can't remember when he's felt so nervous, like a schoolboy waiting to be driven to pick up the most popular girl in school. Today he is going to meet the woman who took a piece of his heart more than forty years ago and never returned it. And maybe never will.

He scrutinizes the lines around his eyes. The deep crinkles attest to what he calls his "geezer status" but they also belie a life filled with joy and laughter. He's fit and healthy, if you don't include the deteriorating heart thankfully still beating in his chest. He wonders what she'll think of how he looks, but then it probably won't matter to her. This meeting means more to him than it ever could for her. She did not come looking for him. His air force training has kept him in great shape. There's no flesh hanging over his belt, thank God, he thinks, and no wattles under his chin.

He's not sure how this visit is going to turn out but he knows it will be one of the most important weeks of his life. Whatever happens he also knows he will die a happy man, having seen Angelique one last time. Throughout his life he has been haunted by the memory of watching her walk away from him and can see the look on her face as if it were yesterday. Now, in a couple of hours he will watch her walk back into it. He checks his tie again and takes a deep breath. He is about to see his past collide with the present and future.

The twenty minute drive to the airport takes almost fifty. He parks in the closest lot, grabs the bouquet of white roses he picked up from a florist and heads to arrivals outside the immigration area. It suddenly occurs to him that he might not recognize her, nor she him. For a moment he panics, then realizes there's not much he can do but closely scrutinize the face of every woman who walks down the airport corridor.

After the first twenty or thirty women walk past he gets somewhat concerned. Maybe she has changed her mind. He looks around. There's no one whose face jogs his memory. He begins to feel like a loser groom left at the altar. Just when he starts to wonder if he should head for the exit he sees another group of passengers coming around the bend in the corridor.

He recognizes her in an instant. The familiarity of her takes his breath away. In one glance he takes in her ivory dress pants, gold shirt and Ivory jacket, gold high heel sandals, her long blond hair tied back in a clip at the nape of her neck and her face with its perfect skin and high cheek bones.

He sees her looking through the waiting crowd. As he lifts his hand to wave she is standing in front of him. He is thrilled she recognizes him. Relieved in fact. His paralyzed lips begin to move.

"I would know you anywhere Angelique. It's almost scary how you have not changed."

"I'd know you too. You look wonderful."

Then she is in his arms. Hugging him the way she used to. He knows it isn't really the same but for that moment he chooses to believe it is. He smells her perfume and the fresh scent of her hair. It makes him strangely want to cry. The joy of it is more than he'd imagined and it suddenly frightens him. She moves away, holding him at arm's length. It's a good thing because he so badly wants to kiss her passionately. He loved kissing her. He hands her the roses and she thanks him.

"Shall we?"

She takes his arm as they walk through the airport and out to the car, with him pulling her suitcase. It's all so surreal for him and a sudden memory of the passion of the last time they were together rushes over him. He concentrates on controlling feelings he thought would have been banished by the passage of more than four decades. Seeing her now in the flesh clearly shows him that time is of little consequence when he comes to his love for this woman he still wants so badly.

"If you had on your uniform you'd hardly look any different. Except for the silver hair. But you still have lots of it."

We laugh. The strangeness of it all is helped by the old familiar banter that often had us howling with laughter. She talks about the large man sitting next to her who kept apologizing that his body wanted to spill over onto her seat, and the newly married couple returning from their honeymoon threatening each other with divorce.

"You're still best storyteller I've ever known."

"You were always a good listener."

"I loved your poetry."

"You were always kind about my poetry. Even when I knew it wasn't very good you tried not to hurt my feelings. I've written better stuff since those days."

We get to the car and I put her suitcase in the trunk.

"You travel light."

"Airports are not friendly places anymore. I try to get on and off planes and out of them as quickly as possible. I'm glad you have a convertible. It just seems the right kind of car to drive in California."

"Most Californians think the same, as you will see once we're on the freeway. I've booked a lunch reservation at one of my favourite restaurants. Are you hungry?"

"In that way I've certainly not changed. I'm always hungry."

"It still doesn't show. You look amazing. As beautiful as I remember."

"That's generous of you. You must also remember how hideous I once looked."

"You were never hideous Angelique. Not to me. You were, and you are, the most beautiful woman I have ever known."

She turns to look at me. Her dark green eyes make me blink and stare at the road. I don't know what's coming.

"That's very kind of you Mark but you're remembering a teenager. You also had a beautiful wife. Angeline showed me photos of her."

"Yes. Margie was a beautiful woman. And a wonderful woman."

"Angeline looks very much like her."

"I know. She's very special to me. My grandson is the joy of my life. What about you? Children? Grandchildren?"

"I have two sons. Both are married, one with a daughter and a son, the other has two sons.

"Yes, of course. Angeline and Paul met your granddaughter at your home. I hear she's quite the young woman."

"Ah, she is that. She's one of a kind. There's never a dull moment when she's around."

On the drive from the airport her tales about her granddaughter keep the mood light hearted. He concentrates on driving and lets her still familiar voice drift over him the way he used to during their long conversations in Bermuda. He knows he shouldn't but he pretends she has come back to him, that this is their time. It's a dangerous notion but he tells himself as long as he doesn't burden her with his pretence it will be OK.

He parks his silver Audi and helps Angelique from the car. He offers his arm. Hank, the owner of Le Grand Cafe, is a close friend and he can't wait to see the look on his face when he walks in with Angelique. Mark has already given him an abbreviated version of their relationship. As soon as they walk in the door Hank is at their side leading them to a table overlooking the Cafe's vast gardens. He gets them seated then leaves to send over a bottle of champagne. He returns, continues the conversation they'd been having and stands around long enough to be asked to join them.

"I don't want to impose. Thank you." He sits. Good friend though he is, for the next fifteen minutes I want to wire his mouth shut. He is enamoured and fawning and monopolizes the conversation. He studiously avoids eye contact but when coffee arrives I manage to catch his eye and give him a laser stare that tells him to get lost.

"Well, I've taken too much of your time. So glad to have met you Angelique. Have a wonderful stay in California. Perhaps we can get together." He sees the look on my face. "Or perhaps not…" He takes Angelique's hand and kisses it in the way of a Frenchman. I want to kill him.

"Your friend's a talker."

"He doesn't know how to take a hint."

We both start to laugh.

"Not too subtle is he? But he has been a good friend for more than twenty years."

"He is certainly entertaining."

"It's almost three. Why don't I get you to your hotel so that you can have a rest before dinner. I thought we'd go to the Officer's Club on base. Do you mind? They have a great chef."

"It sounds wonderful. And I would be glad to have a rest. You have to get to the airport so early now before a flight it adds hours to your travel time."

As they leave, Hank hurries over to say goodbye and presents Angelique with a small gold gift box containing three truffles, a Cafe specialty. They all laugh at his transparency. Conversation on the drive to the Embassy Suites hotel is relaxed and funny. It's as though Angelique senses Mark's need to be personal and helps him avoid it. He drops her off and asks her to be ready by 7 p.m. She kisses him on the cheek and he watches her walk in to the hotel. Driving away he is filled with a myriad of emotions. He's 27 and humming "Some Enchanted Evening."

" Boy, am I setting myself up for another fall."

DALLAS

"How do you think it's going?"

"I have no idea. Fine, I'm sure."

Paul has started counting the number of times I've asked that question since declaring "Angelique's plane has landed in Lompoc." I pray the visit has gotten off to a good start.

"I'm scared for Dad, afraid of the stress this could put on his heart."

"I would venture to say that any stress on his heart will be outweighed by the joy of seeing Angelique. He's got this more under control than you do. Calm yourself or you'll be the one with a cardiac problem."

"Think I'll make tea."

LOMPOC

Mark intended to take a nap. He wanted to be fresh and ready to impress Angelique but he can't turn off his mind. The nice part of him is thrilled to see her looking so beautiful. The jealous part is almost disappointed because there is no getting away from the fact he has never stopped loving her.

Sitting on the patio in the cool, late afternoon he questions the sanity of what he is doing to himself. In four days she will walk out of his life again and for an instant the very thought of it is asphyxiating and he almost chokes on the pain. His heart begins to race and he can feel it thud from his chest up into his throat. Oh great, the first evening he is about to spend with Angelique in more than forty years and he's about to give himself a heart attack.

That thought ruptures his self-defeating reverie. He breathes deeply. Long slow breaths that bring his heart rate back to normal. He gives himself a mental shake. What is wrong with him? He knows there is no way he would miss seeing Angelique. Whatever happens. Damn it he knows what's going to happen. His problem is that he wants to change it, wants her to realize what she missed by leaving him. In the deep recesses of his mind he's hoping she will choose never to leave him again.

If he doesn't get this under control Angelique will be leaving on the next plane. He doesn't want to scare her away and if he starts with the needy, choose me routine she'll be offended, and that's the last thing he wants. The clock on the mantelpiece chimes. He glances up. He has an hour before picking her up and heads to the shower. This is one evening he won't screw up and it had better be the best acting job of his life.

She is waiting when he walks into the lobby of the Embassy Suites, stands up and comes to meet him. She is dressed in a pale green linen two-piece suit with ivory shoes and handbag. Her long blond hair is pulled back and tied with a black ribbon. Then she is hugging him and his heart races.

"You look beautiful."

"You look pretty good yourself. Of course nothing beats that blue uniform you used to wear." She laughs and takes my arm as we head to the car.

"Do you remember you used to run your finger over my wings and say…"

"Fly safely, Flyboy. Of course I remember."

"It was my good luck charm."

"Well, I'm glad if it kept you safe."

On the short drive to the Vandenberg air base we talk about Lompoc. She has read about the historic small town and has many questions, most of which I was glad I could actually answer.

As we drive through the Vandenberg gate there's a feeling of familiarity. Angelique feels it too.

"It's been a long time since we drove onto a base together. We were so young," she laments.

"Hard to believe how long. I finally understand what my parents were talking about when they used to say don't wish your life away and that time passes quicker when you get older."

"We become our parents before we know it. Of course we all vow that will never happen."

Walking in to the Officer's Mess I greet old friends and introduce Angelique. I can tell they are all wanting to know the story behind my date. The Mess hostess leads us to seats in the lounge where we've decided to have a cocktail before dinner. Even though I am functioning in the present, my mind and heart is determined to sneak back to those days on Kindley, to pretend nothing has changed. I keep giving my brain a silent shake, noting to myself that if I keep this up I'll be certifiable by the end of the evening.

Then the waiter is standing before us.

"Is it still dark Bacardi with half a lime, coke and ice?"

"You remember what I drink?"

"You used to laugh and say it was a 'genetic' drink for a Canadian."

"Still do." We laugh, then remember the waiter.

I repeat Angelique's drink order and ask for double scotch and water.

By the time we finish our drinks Angelique has filled in the years since we parted. I am fascinated but not surprised by any of it.

"Your turn. I've been doing all the talking." Before I can respond the waiter returns to tell us our table in the dining room is ready. I take her arm. I'm cock of the walk. I'm pathetic. Oh well. Over dinner it's my turn to recount what's happened in my life.

"I did two tours in Vietnam. Those were hard times. I lost a dozen or more friends in that God forsaken place. Do you remember Sammy Price and Joe Green?" She nods. "They were killed two days after we arrived on the first tour. I saw their 'coptors get hit and go down in front of me. It was all happening fast but it seemed like everything started going in slow motion. I have to confess I'd never been so terrified in my life as I was in that moment. It really hit home that we were all vulnerable and no one was guaranteed a safe ride. Jim Hicks was killed at the end of the war. I took one hit in the first tour and three the second time around. The odds weren't looking good and I was sure glad we pulled out before I got sent back a third time."

"I can't imagine what that's like. And I can't imagine what our lives would be like if there were not young men willing to put themselves in harm's way in those damn wars. I often thank God for the bravery of men and women who go to war. It enrages me when I hear civilians complaining about them or condemning them because they're killing people. It's war for heaven's sake. And one thing that's patently clear when you listen to them ranting and raving is that they would never risk their lives for anyone. Yet, if they were threatened they'd want those same brave men and women to be out there killing the bad guys. They're such hypocrites I can hardly stand to listen to them."

Mark begins to laugh.
"You find this funny?"

"No. No. Angelique you really haven't changed." She looks over at him, stares and starts laughing.

"I was doing this for hours on end in the Islander, wasn't I? How often did we lose track of time and Leo would be waiting for us to shut up so that he could close the place and go home."

"Considering he kept drinking beer while he waited we may have ruined his liver. We knew some interesting characters back then."

"We did. I regret losing touch with my roommates. I've always meant to track down Bridget and Jessie. I heard Jessie died many years ago in an accident. They both were such wonderful friends. They saved my life."

"You went through a very difficult time during those last months you were in Bermuda. There were days when we were so worried you wouldn't make it because of the illnesses. Or that you might decide you couldn't take any more."

"You actually discussed that?"

"Yes. We did. If things had not changed and you had not started to recover we were going to do what today would be called an 'intervention,' including calling your parents."

"I'm really glad things went the way they did. I have to admit I was at the end of my rope and almost ended it all. I still can't believe I even thought such a thing. But I was pretty desperate."

"Looking at you no one would even know what you suffered."

"As I've said many times, I am a very lucky woman. Many people never recover completely from Bell's Palsy. Then there was that damn smallpox vaccination. Well, anyway. It was a long time ago. I really should contact Bridget."

"Speaking of tracking people down. You've been very kind about all of this. It must seem pretty bizarre and I'm still amazed you didn't tell Angeline and Paul, and me, to get lost and for me in particular, to get a life and leave you alone."

"I must say I did find it somewhat strange that you wanted to see me after so many years. But I was also flattered and touched that you had fond memories of me, a girl who walked away when you were offering your heart to her. You know that was one of the most difficult nights of my life."

"I'm really glad to hear you say that. I've often wondered, agonized, about how you were feeling when you walked away that night. I was hurting so badly and wanted you more than I've ever wanted anything or anyone in my life. I couldn't accept that it may have meant nothing to you."

"It hurt Mark. More than I wanted to admit to myself. I was so tempted to stay and I struggled with the guilt of having hurt you for a long time."

"I told you that night I would never stop loving you and I never have. I won't pretend that I don't still love you Angelique, but I will say it tonight and I promise not to bring it up again. I know you love your husband and even though I might fantasize about what might have been or could be. I am also realistic. I am truly grateful you are generous enough to give me these few days with you."

"I'm glad to be here, Mark. You were a special man in my life and I couldn't refuse to come to see you."

"Did Angeline tell you …?"

"About your heart? Yes. I'm sorry. You look so healthy."

"Yeah. That's the frustrating part. I feel great, unless I overdo things and my heart starts acting up."

"Are you eligible for a transplant?"

"I'm in a Catch 22 situation unfortunately. Even though my heart could fail any moment and they have me on the transplant list I have to get much worse to get a heart and the bad news is I may not survive getting worse. I don't expect I'll be so lucky to survive long enough to get some other poor soul's heart."

"You seem to have a good attitude about it all."

"I have to. I know the odds. That's one reason I wanted to find you. Before the curtain comes down I wanted to see you one last time, to be able to tell you that I didn't stop loving you."

"Mark…"

"I'm sorry Angelique but I have to say it. I've been waiting over forty years. Please take it in the way it's meant and don't think I expect anything from you. Not that I wouldn't wish … but I know what I've done is also very selfish. I justify it by telling myself it's a dying man's last wish."

"Oh Mark."

"It may sound maudlin but I know it's probably the truth. So, now I've got that off my chest let's just enjoy ourselves, two old friends sharing memories and laughing. "

"Works for me."

Dessert arrives and the band begins to play.

"Would you like to dance? They're playing your song."

"You planned this. How many bands today are playing Some Enchanted Evening?"

She laughs and gets up from her chair. I am making memories tonight. As I take her in my arms and we move across the floor I silently thank Rodgers and Hammerstein for their beautiful song. This is as close as I can get to her and I am savouring every second. The song ends and the band immediately starts to play Pat Boone's hit, Love Letters in the Sand. Angelique pulls away from me, looks questioningly, shakes her head and smiles. She knows I am not so subtly trying to recreate a night like those we often spent together in Bermuda. She sighs and relaxes in my arms. She will never be mine but for this one night on the dance floor I can pretend.

We talk and dance until I begin to feel tired. She is concerned and insists we sit out the last set. Even though we've been restricting our jiving to the slower version of the dance, the unusual exercise is exhausting. I come clean and confess I arranged to have the band play many of her favourite songs from our days in Bermuda. The band leader announces "Last dance ladies and gentlemen." As the music starts I get up and hold out my hand.

"You didn't arrange this one as well?"

"I swear this one was not my doing. It really is a coincidence."

I am as surprised as she is to hear the song One Kiss for Old Time's Sake by the Righteous Brothers. It's another we'd danced to many times. As we circle the floor it feels like a last dance and I know she is feeling it too. I can tell because when I draw her closer than I have a right to, she doesn't resist.

Near the end of the song I raise my head from her hair and as if in slow motion lower my lips to meet her mouth. She doesn't stop me. The kiss has a tenderness that soon turns to fire and I begin to feel the passion of that long ago kiss. I feel her heart race and the intensity of the passion threatens public decency.

The music ends before the kiss. She pulls her body away, shaken, as I am. We slowly walk back to our table. Everything is the same but somehow different. There's an electricity and tension between us and I find numerous small ways to constantly touch her. People I know come to chat and around midnight we drive back to her hotel. I brace myself for the invitation that will never come.

"Don't get out. Thank you for a wonderful, memorable evening. I've had so much fun."

"Me too." I want to kiss her again. Want to walk her to her room, be invited in and make love to her to assuage a longing that's no less urgent than it was forty years ago. I can tell she knows what I'm thinking and feels uncomfortable. Her discomfort pains me and I get myself under control. She sees my grip on the steering wheel relax. She smiles.

"What's the plan for tomorrow?"

"Angeline, Paul and David are arriving in the morning. They'll be staying for a few days so that they can see you and be here to see Roni and your husband." I almost choke on the word. "Angeline wants to know if you'd like to have lunch with her and do some shopping."

"I'd love that." She leans over, kisses me on the cheek. "It really has been a wonderful night. I will never forget it. See you tomorrow."

"Sleep well." I watch her walk pass the doorman and speak to him as he opens the door. I wait. She turns and waves. My heart leaves my mouth. Now I can leave.

Angelique wakes in the morning rested and hungry. Taking a quick shower she dresses and heads to the restaurant of the hotel. She would like to find a quaint place to eat but her stomach demands food and her exploring can wait until lunchtime.

Reading the local newspaper, courtesy of the concierge, over a breakfast of oatmeal, eggs, bacon and toast, she finds it hard to concentrate on the vagaries of life in this small California town. As much as she tried not to last night, she kept letting herself be pulled back into the past. Mark had not changed. He is still the sweet, funny, attentive and caring man she remembers from those Bermuda days.

She is also feeling guilty about the kiss. It seemed like the right thing at the time and if she was being honest, impossible to stop. But she hopes Mark didn't read something into it that she can't deliver. It is also the first time she has kissed another man on the lips since she met Jon and part of her feels disloyal to him. Another part remembers the sexual tension from that last kiss in Bermuda and if she's really honest, that feeling was almost enough to betray loyalties last night when Mark kissed her on the dance floor. She vowed not to put herself in a vulnerable position again while she is here.

She is glad Angeline and her family would be visiting for the next couple of days until Jon and Roni arrive. Mark is too much of a temptation. It was somewhat intoxicating to feel nineteen again. She decides to go for a long walk and explore a little before Angeline arrived at 2.

"So what do you think of her? Has she changed? Been having fun? What did you do last night?"

"She's wonderful. She's not changed. Yes, I'm, we're having fun and I took her to the Officer's Mess last night. No more questions or discussion. Except for me to thank you both again for finding her and bringing her here. There are no words..."

"That's OK Dad. We know. What did she…?"

"Mom, gramps said no more questions."

"Angel, please?"

"Sorry Dad. I'm so used to prying." We all laugh. "Did you ask Angelique about shopping?"

"Yes, and she's looking forward to it. You can take my car. Joe and Emma across the street are in Europe and if either of us need to we can take their car. I'm dog sitting."

Angelique and Angeline greet each other like old friends, a genuine feeling on both sides. They explore dozens of quaint shops in the town, visit the local mall, take several tea breaks and shop again. The last shop they visit is one owned by one of Angeline's old school friends.

"Ang hi! Haven't seen you in a while. How are you?"

They hug.

"I'm great. We've been too busy to come out here as often as we'd like. Teresa, I'd like you to meet Angelique. She's a friend from Montreal."

"Nice to meet you. I'd love to visit Montreal. It's as close to Paris as I'll ever get. What do you think of Lompoc? It's not Montreal."

"It's beautiful and I'm glad it's not Montreal," she says laughing and making a new friend.

"Wow, I just realized how similar your names are – Angeline. Angelique. What a coincidence."

The two look at each other.

"Yes, isn't it? Although Angeline has the youth advantage." The awkward moment ends.

"Well, look around. We have four rooms – over there are dresses and skirts, over there jackets, coats and boots, here as you can see is the lingerie and the last room has accessories. I make the place sound huge don't I?"

"It's a beautiful boutique."

"Come on, let's shop."

They explore the first three rooms and both find many "must have" or "just want" items. The piles on the front counter are growing, much to Teresa's delight. She offers them tea and biscuits before they tackle the last room. The talkative boutique owner clearly wants more information about Angelique but good manners keep her from asking outright and the two women, sensing her curiosity, are not willing to oblige.

After a twenty minute break they're in the jewelry section, both finding "must haves." The scarf and hat section is somewhat jumbled and as they search through the shelves they both see it at the same time. A pink hat. Neither moves nor speaks. Angeline is picturing the hat from the trunk. Angelique is remembering the last time she wore it.

"He has it you know." Angelique turns to stare.

"What?"

"Dad has your pink hat. He's kept it hidden in a trunk in our attic."

"Your mother?"

"She knew."

"This is so awkward."
"Please don't let it be. Life is what it is. It's part of Dad's life and I've accepted it. My mother accepted it."

"You are remarkable people."

"Not really Angelique. We're just trying to make the best of life. It may be clichéd but we're not here for a long time."

"So might as well make it a good time." They laugh and the tension between them evaporates. They add scarves and jewelry and ask Teresa to "add it all up," which she does happily
.

"Thank you Ang for bringing Angelique in. Don't be a stranger."

"Bye Teresa. I'm really glad you're doing well."

"Well, she'll have no problem meeting her overheads this month."

"Your name will be golden and so will mine for bringing you there. Let's get all of this in the car and head home to see what the men have planned for dinner. They're cooking."

The evening is filled with good conversation and much laughter. The Texas ribs, baked potato and salad make a successful dinner and the men are relieved. Angelique and David share a love of planes and he confides that he has not told his parents but will soon be letting them know he has applied to the Air Force Academy.

"I want to follow in gramp's footsteps."

"Will they be pleased?"

"I hope so. I think so."

"I wish you success. You have a good role model."

David looks across the room at his grandfather. "Yes. I do. Gramps is a great guy."

Angelique notices that Mark is looking tired. Worried, she feigns exhaustion from the shopping.

"If you don't mind, I'll say goodnight and get back to the hotel."

"I'll drive you."

"No Dad, you sit tight. I picked her up, I'll return her safe and sound."

Mark doesn't argue. Another sign he is tired. It's noted by all of them.

"We're planning lunch at the Cafe and an afternoon at the beach tomorrow. Would that work for you Angelique?"

"Sounds exactly what I'd like. Thank you all for being so welcoming."

Mark's goodnight hug is heartfelt, but Angelique can feel his fatigue. "Get some rest OK?" Mark nods and doesn't protest.

"I will. See you tomorrow."

The flashing red light on the phone tells her she has a message and she quickly checks to find out Jon has called. He'll be up until midnight. She dials the hotel number he has left.

"Is this my Angelique?"

"It will always be your Angelique."

"How are you sweetheart? Having fun?"

"I am. The Wintertons are a wonderful family."

"Will I like Flyboy?"

"You will. And he'll like you. He won't want to but he will." We laugh the laughter of two people who know each other so well there's no need for words. Jon talks about the success of his book tour and the characters who come to the book signings. We talk for more than an hour.

"I'm going to let you go to sleep. You'll want to look good for your flyboy at the beach tomorrow," he says, with a tiny hint of jealously. "And I will see you the day after tomorrow."

"I'll be so glad to see you Jon. I love you."

"I know you do and I love you more than anything in the world sweetheart."

"nite." "nite."

The weather cooperates and their day at the beach is perfect. Angelique and Mark decide to go for a walk on the sand. Paul, Angeline and David watch them walk away.

"Look at her. I want to have a body like that when I'm her age."

"No problem, Angel. Look at you now." He leans over and kisses her on the lips.

"Get a room you two."

"So David, what do you think of Angelique?"

"She's great. Too bad she's married. Gramps sure has the hots for her."

"David!"

"Mom, you'd have to be deaf and blind to not to see the way he looks at her all the time, especially when she's not looking. But I have to give him credit for not letting her see it and embarrassing her. I can understand it though. She must have really been something when gramps met her."

"That's the person he still sees."

"Her husband arrives tomorrow doesn't he?"

"Yes and her granddaughter Roni is flying in an hour after his plane lands."

"And why is she coming here?"

"She told your mother she wants to see the U.S. She seems to have an affinity for the U.S. and Americans."

"That's a change from most Canadians isn't it? They seem to often say pretty nasty things about us."

"Not all Canadians."

"What's she like, Dad?"

"Very much like her grandmother or G'mere as she calls her. Her energy level is scary and meeting her will give you a glimpse into what she'll be like in fifty years. She's the walking incarnation of Angelique, wouldn't you say Angel?"

Mark is quiet. He gets up and strolls along the beach.

"Absolutely. Would you mind if we invite the three of them to Texas for a few days? If they want to visit."

"Not at all. Here they come. Your dad seems tired. Happy but tired."

"I've noticed and so did Angelique last night. I'm sure that's why she left when she did. We'll have to keep an eye on him. Would you mind taking Angelique to the airport tomorrow to meet Jon and Roni? Dad will offer but …"

"I hear you. I'll take care of it."

148

After a day at the beach everyone agrees that pizza on the deck is the preferred dinner option. Their conversation is easy and Mark has to remind himself she's not his wife, but the temptation is overwhelming. He knows it can go nowhere. Close to 11 p.m. she insists it's time for her to get some sleep. He knows she can see his exhaustion and can sense his reluctance to bring the evening to an end. He walks her out to the car to wait for Paul to drive her to the hotel.

"It's been a perfect day, Mark. Thank you. You and your family are so wonderful to me."

"You feel like family Angelique. Does that sound odd?"

"In a way. But not really. I suppose it's because we've actually known each other for over forty years, despite not seeing each other. You know Mark you have been a lucky man to have had a wife like Margie and a daughter like Angeline. Their love for you has been extraordinary. Not many wives or daughters would understand…"

"I know that Angelique. I often find myself conflicted, knowing how much Margie loved me despite her knowing she shared my heart with another woman."

"But she had you and from what Angeline has told me she never had a reason to doubt your love."

"Thank you for that. Well, the next time I see you it will be with your husband and granddaughter."

"I think you'll like them."

"I'm sure I'll like your granddaughter." He laughs in spite of himself. "I'll try to like Jon. He's loved you and taken care of you, how can I not like him."

"You're a fine man, Mark Forrester. Here's Paul. See you tomorrow."

At the airport Paul is glad Mark is not there to see Angelique greet her husband. There is no doubt about how those two feel about each other. That's how I want us to be, he tells himself, thinking about Angeline. Angelique remembers he's also there.

"Paul, I'm sorry. Jon, Roni, you remember Paul." They shake hands, pleased to meet again.

"Nice to see again Mr. Winterton."

"Paul, please."

"I love California already."

"You haven't left the airport yet."

"I loved it from the plane window G'pere. I may never leave." Paul leads the way to the baggage area. Their conversation is lively and noisy on the drive to the hotel, mainly because of Roni and her non-stop chatter.

"I'll pick you up around 6. Mark has booked dinner at the Blacksmith restaurant. Is that time good for you?"

"That's great Paul. Thank you for your hospitality."

"My pleasure Jon. See you later."

"Oh, is this dress up or down?"

"More up than down but not formal."

"OK. Thanks."

"Let's get settled in our rooms and have tea. Is there a place for tea G'mere?"

"Yes. The restaurant here in the hotel also has delicious tea biscuits."

"Awesome. Let's hurry. I want to know everything." Angelique and Jon exchange an amused look.

"Don't say it. I know she's like me."

"Come on G'pere. You want to hear it all too."

"I'm beginning to wonder if it wasn't a mistake inviting you two to join me."

Over tea Angelique recounts her visit so far, at least most of it. Roni has a thousand questions and their loud laughter draws amused glances from the dozen or so other guests at nearby tables. Their familiarity is a balm to the emotional tension she's experienced over the past few days.

"Well, I could do with a lie down. I'm not as young as I'd like to be. How about you sweetheart? Want a rest with your husband?"

"Let's go. What about you Roni?"

"Ah, don't worry about me. I am as young as I wish. I'm going for a walk to check the place out."

"Don't walk too far. Call if you get lost. Don't look at me like that young lady. I'm your grandfather and I'm allowed to be concerned."

"I'll call, if necessary. See you later." She gives each of them a peck on the cheek and saunters out of the room, surrounded by an air of confidence.

"She's really something. The man who ends up in her life will never suffer a moment of boredom. Although he might laugh himself to death, which is not a bad way to go. Now about that lie down…" Jon takes Angelique's hand and they walk to the elevator, in anticipation.

Angelique opens her eyes. "What are you staring at? I could feel you staring."

"Two eyes, a nose, mouth…" He laughs and kisses her.

"Before you start that again, what time is it?"

"Just five. Lots of time."

"For you maybe. I'm taking a leisurely bath."

"Coming."

"I said leisurely."

"Darn. I'll have a quick shower, then, I'll run your bath."

"Sounds great. I'll watch the news. And take a rain check. "

The phone rings at 6. Paul is waiting in the lobby.

"How do I look?"

"You look quite handsome. Why?"

"Well, I'm about to meet the competition and I want to make sure I look good."

"It's all in your mind. Call your granddaughter and tell her to meet us in the lobby. Immediately."

Walking in to the restaurant Angelique is stressing. She crosses her fingers, hoping the two men who love her like each other. Mark, Angeline and David get up to greet them. Mark and Jon size each other up, seem to like what they see and she relaxes. David and Roni seem to have an understanding and love of flight in common and tune out the adults whenever they find the conversation boring. It feels like a family reunion with bizarre overtones. Overall, they get away with an evening of carefree banter and no disasters. They all agree to spend the following day sightseeing and taking a tour of the Vandenberg air base. Even the two teenagers.

"He's a great guy," Mark whispers as he gives her a goodnight hug. "I wish I could dislike him."

Back in the hotel Angelique and Jon decide to have a nightcap in the bar. Roni joins them.

"I wish I could dislike him."

"Really? That's what he said about you."

"Really?" They both laugh.

"So am I to deduce you don't hate Flyboy, G'pere?"

"You never beat around the bush do you Roni? No, I don't hate him. He's an intelligent, interesting and likeable man. And besides, he has great taste in women."

"What about you Roni. Did you have a good time? What did you think of David?"

"I had a great time G'mere. I like your flyboy. He's not G'pere but he's a nice guy. David's OK. Well, I'm off to bed. What time are we having breakfast and what time are we being picked up? I wasn't listening."

"Breakfast at eight and pickup at ten. Is that OK with you?"

"You bet." She hugs them, tells them she loves them and escapes.

"Do you find it odd she didn't want to stay and talk our ears off?"

"Perhaps she's tired. I've never known that to happen but there's a first for everything when it comes to our granddaughter."

"And what about you, my darling? You seem to have survived the evening pretty well. You look tired. Let's take these aging bodies to bed. I'll give you a massage."

"You're a fine wife, sweetheart. Lead on. I'm already imagining your hands on my body."

Sightseeing with Mark and the Wintertons is a great deal of fun. The tour of Vandenberg reminds Angelique of the first time she met Mark and she could tell he was having the same flashbacks. Over lunch in the Officers Mess Roni, never the diplomat, drops a bombshell.

"So, when do we get to see this pink hat?"

They all become a snapshot, frozen in the moment. David breaks first.

"Are all young Canadians rude or is it just you?"

Roni is taken aback. She looks around the table at the stricken faces and for the first time in her short, outspoken life, realizes it may be time to learn some modicum of restraint. Yet, she also refuses to back down.

"You may consider it rude and I'm sorry if there's any offence to be taken here. But, let's face it, we're all here because of a pink hat. And I'm only saying what the elephant in the room here is. Any friend of mine just has to accept that I speak my mind." The last jibe is directed pointedly at David.

"That may be but there's a difference between being outspoken and damned rude."

Mark recovers and realizing this exchange could escalate, calls a truce.

"Roni may have given us all a bit of a shock for the moment but she is quite right. Angelique's pink hat has indeed brought all of us together and if it's OK with her, I will take the hat from its box when we return to the house."

"I confess I would like to see it. I know it sounds strange but I have so often wondered whatever happened to that hat. I expected it would end up in a landfill after all these years."

"I'm sorry G'mere. Guess those good manners you taught me didn't take too well." She includes everyone in her second "Sorry." The waiter arrives to present dessert choices and the hat conversation is lost in discussions about Crème Brule, dark fudge chocolate cake and apple pie. Angelique realizes both Jon and Mark are watching her. She ignores them both.

"Angeline, you were asking if we could come to visit you in Texas for a few days and we've all decided to take you up on your kind offer. Roni has had a fixation with your Lone Star state, so, if your offer is still open, the answer is yes. Thank you."

Conversation now centres on the Texas visit, changing flights, sightseeing and length of stay. Instead of flying home to Montreal the next day they would be flying to Dallas on a late evening flight. Roni is almost giddy with excitement and turns to ask David what young people do for entertainment in Texas. Before she can form the words she notes his silence, and then watches a frown cross his face before he excuses himself from the table. It gives her a sinking feeling in the pit of her stomach. That damn hat, she thinks, and my big mouth.

If anyone notices a chill in the air around the young people during the rest of the sightseeing day they don't draw attention to it. Roni and David barely exchange words but manage to be civil when they do.

It's decided that a farewell dinner should be prepared at home where they can all relax away from the formality of a restaurant. Angeline takes charge and everyone is given a chore. Once the main preparations are under way Mark serves drinks in the living room, leaves and returns with a large white box.

"Roni, I know you're feeling badly about having brought up the pink hat, but don't. This is not just any pink hat. It belongs to a very special lady we all care very much about." He removes the hat from the box and gives it to Angelique.

"It's exactly as I remember it. I also remember the pink checked sun

154

dress I wore with it the day Bridget and I toured Kindley." Then, addressing the hat, "Do you have any idea what a commotion you've caused?" Mark extends a hand helping her off the low couch. She walks to the mirror above the fireplace, lifts the hat and places it on her still blond hair.

"Sweetheart that is definitely your hat."

"G'mere, you look fabulous."

"OK Dad, now I know why you've had this image in your head all these years," Angeline says jokingly.

Mark attempts to join the levity, enough to fool them all, but his heart is too heavy and threatens to choke him. He retreats to another place in time and moments of their days together in Bermuda flit across his memory. He begs the universe to restore his equilibrium. He does not want them to see his pain and exquisite joy. He reminds himself that this won't be the last time he'll see her. It helps. It also makes things worse.

"The hat is back where it belongs. You're as beautiful in it as you were when you first owned it."

They all applaud and his heart beats more calmly.

"Well, now that the Pink Secret is a secret no longer, let's eat." Angeline's announcement takes them all into the dining room.
Later that night Angelique sits in front of the hotel room mirror, dressed in cotton pajamas and her pink hat. She never thought she would see it again. Wearing it feels good but also reminds her of the passage of time. Can it really have been so long ago? How did youth disappear so quickly? Lost in reverie she didn't hear Jon return to the room.

"If you look this good now in your pink hat I can really understand why Mark was besotted. Going to bed in it?" He laughs and kisses the back of her neck. "I won't mind sleeping with you and that famous pink hat."

"I'll pass, but I appreciate the offer. That is I'll leave the hat off but I will take you up on the coming to bed offer. I love you so much Jon. I don't ever want to make you feel uncomfortable and I don't ever want you to be hurt."

"I'm fine. I have you and your love. And now I also have a pink hat."

He pulls Angelique down on the bed. "Come on sweetheart, let's get under the duvet. I'm feeling energetic. Must be that pink hat."

The next afternoon they are all at the airport, all of them saying good-bye to Mark. Angelique is acutely aware of his emotional turmoil which he is struggling to conceal. She leaves the conversation she is only half paying attention to between Angeline and Roni, who appears to get along with Angeline as well as she does with her mother and G'mere, and sits next to Mark.

"It's difficult when you're the only one not travelling. I'm sorry we're all leaving at the same time."

Mark looks at her without speaking for several seconds. Then, slowly takes her hand.

"You have no idea. You walking away again is almost as hard as it was the first time. I should be getting use to it."

"Perhaps it would have been better if I had not come here."

"No. Forgive me. I'm just feeling sorry for myself. I would endure any amount of hurt to have seen you again. I have to tell you it all seems surreal. Most sane people would consider this whole situation something…"

"Out of a novel. I know. I've thought that myself." They both laugh and the tension eases.

"Did you take your hat?"

"Oh, no. I left the box on the dining room table after breakfast. It seems that hat doesn't want to leave you."

"You'll just have to come back for it. I hope you enjoy Texas. It's a very interesting state. Angeline and Paul are delighted you've agreed to spend a few days with them. Though to do justice to even a small part of Texas you need longer than three days."

"As a matter of fact that's the conclusion we've come to so if they'll have us we thought we'd extend our stay to about ten days. Roni told us it was 'absolute lunacy' to schedule a visit to Texas for only three days. You've probably gathered she has a way of getting around her grandparents, so we gave in and agreed to stay longer."

"I've noticed a bit of the frigid treatment between her and David. What do you suppose that's about?"

"They're teenagers. And they're both trying to be in charge of the friendship."

"They are certainly both opinionated. I spent several hours the other night just listening. My two cents worth would have not only been unwelcome but also quite irrelevant, given the intensity of their political discussion that degenerated into a Russian standoff."

"I imagine we'll have an interesting stay, given that David is on his own territory."

When they are not expected to take part in family activities, David plays the welcoming host introducing Roni to his friends, taking her to parties and typical teen hang out spots, particularly the beach and music venues. Most days they hang out at the beach with several of David's friends. One morning as they walk along the beach from the parking lot they are unusually silent. There's an undefined tension in the air between them and it's uncomfortable. David breaks the silence.

"Why do you call your grandmother gee mere?"

"You've seen her. She is not a grandmother. She doesn't look the part nor act the part and none of us would dare call her grandmother. That's how she refers to herself and that's what we call her."

"You're very like her."

"So I've been told. Is that good or bad?"

"Why are you called Roni?"

"I hate Rhonda. Nice name. Not me."

"Oh."

There's more silence. Roni feels confused. For some odd, aggravating reason her eyes fill with tears and she thanks God for dark glasses. Not wanting to draw attention to her watery orbs she doesn't wipe the tears away, which blurs her vision. She stumbles. David grabs her arm and holds her upright.

"Are you OK?" Roni stares at him.

"Yeah." A sudden flash of molten heat between them makes them jump apart, as if they'd been zapped with lightning.

"Hey David, Roni, over here." *The sound of their friends' voices jostles them out of their trance-like state and they walk over to meet them. Roni doesn't understand what had just happened and doesn't like how uncomfortable it made her feel.*

The three Canadians are as reluctant to leave as their American friends are to let them go. On departure day they console themselves with promises to get together again soon. Jon suggests they drive to Montreal for a visit which would make it possible for Mark to join them. They all agree, and with good bye hugs the three are on their way home. If anyone notices the teenagers' offhand goodbyes they aren't saying.

"Thanks for your hospitality."

"You're welcome. Thanks for coming."

"I appreciated your time. Your friends were fun."

"No problem. Well. Bye."

"Yeah, bye."

Texas is soon receding below the clouds. Angelique and Jon sit together while Roni sits across the aisle. She announces she is going to read, clamps on earphones and ignores everyone except the air attendant who delivers the food.
"Anything wrong with our granddaughter?" Angelique looks across the aisle.

"I'm not sure. If there is we'll eventually hear about it. She's making decisions in that head of hers and you know what she's like – nothing stays a secret for long under that blond hair."

"She told me last night she is definitely applying to universities in the

U.S. She's 'totally' made up her mind."

"Then I'd say her parents will be getting that news soon, if she's not already told them."

"One good thing about her parents, they know never to be surprised by anything she says or does. They always expect the unexpected."

Laughing. "So do we. That's why she keeps us young. Now, I think I'll do a bit of reading myself because I'm sure you're going to want to watch that car chase movie they're showing this evening. Haven't you seen Gone in 60 Seconds Part IV?"

"Your point is?"

MONTREAL

In Montreal life picks up where it has left off, sort of. Angelique and Jon work on their new books and Roni hits the books to ensure her final year of high school produces the marks she needs to get into a U.S. university.

They talk with Angeline and Paul every few weeks and there is a monthly call from Mark. He doesn't talk about his health but Angeline confided that the doctor had increased his medication because his heart had become weaker. If they are out Mark leaves a message with the admonition it isn't necessary to return the call. Sometimes Angelique calls back, sometimes she waits until the next call. As much as she doesn't want to admit it, she looks forward to their conversations.

About ten months after they'd been in Lompoc and Texas Angeline called to ask if it would be convenient for them to come to Montreal for a short visit. Mark was feeling well enough to travel by car and they hoped David might fly up to join them for the weekend. A date is set for five weeks later. Angelique and Jon begin preparations in the house and make plans to make the visit memorable. Because of Mark's deteriorating heart condition Angelique tells herself every conversation, every visit could be the last. She tries to push the thought aside.

The week-long visit is a repeat of the laughter, sightseeing and good eating of their U.S. experience, albeit with a French flavour. David flew in on Friday to join a very large family party on Saturday. Angelique and Jon had invited their two sons and their families to join them and were delighted they could all fix schedules to attend. Their son James, his wife Claire and daughter Roni were driving from the Eastern Townships just outside Montreal Saturday morning and their son Chris, his wife Suzette and twin sons Nicholas and Matthew came from Ottawa Friday night.

Ignoring protestations and admonitions they should all be helping more, at 3 p.m. Angelique sends all of them out for a walk. She wants an hour alone to put finishing touches on the table settings and to make sure her organized menu has nothing missing. The gigantic turkey and its six accompaniments all seem to be at the right stage in the cooking process. The English trifle and chocolate fudge cake stand like peacocks in the fridge. The trifle is large enough to feed them all, but the chocolate cake is Jon's favourite. As she closes the fridge door she hears Mark ask Roni for a third helping of dessert. Then, a flash of memory from another evening In Bermuda.

"Excuse me, I'd like another piece of cake."

"You're eating another piece. You've just had two pounds of chocolate in the last hunk."

"Yes, I'm eating another piece, every bite of it. I might even take a third piece home for later."

She laughs now at the memory. Guess both men will be enjoying the cake. Before heading upstairs to shower and dress for dinner she walks around the table, making sure the place cards are positioned so that everyone has a well matched dinner partner. She and Jon will sit at either end of the table and she knows he won't mind that she has seated Mark on her right. He would be heartbroken to be seated elsewhere. Deciding all is well she pours herself a small glass of fine Port, a gift from Jon, and takes it with her, deciding to definitely forego the shower for a bath.

Before immersing herself in the rose scented water she takes a black Chanel-style shift dress from the closet and pairs it with a red belt and red pumps. She chooses her favouite pearls and earrings and a pearl clip to hold up her hair.

By 6 p.m. they are all gathered in the living room and from the kitchen

Angelique can hear the buzz of conversation and much laughter. Young voices of grandchildren punctuated by enquiries from adults. Then there are the voices of the two men who want her heart. She cherishes them both. She has a sudden, overwhelming feeling this will be a night to remember.

Dinner is a lively affair. There are no wallflowers in the group and conversation never lags. She, Mark and Jon deal with several awkward questions about their relationships and the now famous pink hat, and then the conversation moves on.

At his end of the table Jon is enjoying talking cars with Paul and his older son Chris. At times, while he is listening to them, he glances down the long table to where Angelique is sitting between Mark on one side and their daughter-in-law Suzette on the other. Suzette is often deep in conversation with Angeline, leaving Mark more time to talk with Angelique. Watching, Jon is reminded of the many times he has noticed the way Mark looks at his wife.

Even though Mark tries to control it, there is no hiding his love for her. Occasionally Jon feels a twinge of jealously, then shakes it off, telling himself he will keep Angelique only if she truly wants to be with him. If she wants Mark, that's where she will go. He is banking on their avowed love and friendship to keep them together. As if sensing his scrutiny, Mark looks up and catches his eye. Jon nods and smiles. Mark smiles in return. Damn. If his wife's old love was an unlikable character.

"What made you choose the University of Texas?"

"I checked out the program and the campus and I've always had a hankering to go there. I had a pen pal in elementary school from Austin and decided way back then I would either visit or try to get into school there. You're going to the Air Force Academy?"

Yes, if I had not chosen the AFA I would have enrolled at Texas U. It's a great university. You'll enjoy it there."

"Your parents have invited me for holidays when I can't get home. I hope you don't mind."
"It's their house and they have lots of room."

"Yeah."

Mark turns to speak with Roni and Angelique looks around the table, at the family she loves dearly and the new friends who have quickly wormed themselves into their hearts.

"It's a fine clan, isn't it?" She turns at the sound of Mark's voice and nods in agreement.

"Even if this is all I can ever have of your life Angelique, I thank you. I feel blessed that you and Jon have welcomed all of us into your family. And not in a small way. Jon is a class act."

"You are both so funny. Jon says something similar about you. I guess I just have great taste in men."

"G'mere should I clear the table?"

"That would be lovely, Roni. And I'm sure your cousins and David would be happy to help. The sooner you clear the table the sooner you can bring out dessert."

The four of them erupt from the table and before the end of even the shortest conversation the dishwasher is running, dessert plates are delivered and the trifle and chocolate cake are sitting on the table.

"I have to say that was impressive. Thank you all. For your efforts you can help yourselves before the adults."

Angelique almost laughs out loud when Jon and Mark tell everyone how much they love chocolate fudge cake. Each of them assumes she's made it just for him, which, she thinks to herself, is true. At evening's end, James, Clair and Roni leave for home. Chris, Suzette and their boys are staying the night. Suzette shoos Nicholas and Matthew upstairs to bed and Jon takes everyone else into the living room for after dinner drinks. Angelique heads into the kitchen, having refused offers of help from everyone. Roni and her team have cleared up most of the dinner debris and only dessert plates and cutlery remain for washing

"I insist on helping."

"You really don't have to. There's hardly anything left to do. Roni and the boys did a great job. That girl can stack a dishwasher like no one else I've ever seen."

"It's these little jobs I'll never get to do with you Angelique. Indulge me. I want to have these moments in my memory bank. Why are you laughing?"

"You're an old romantic Mark. It's a loveable trait."

"Can I read more into that than you meant to convey? You know loveable, love me etc…"

"Here, dry." She hands him a dish.

Their chat turns to safer subjects and once they've finished they join the rest of the clan in the living room. Angeline is the first to notice the 1 a.m. chimes of the grandfather clock in the corner. They are all surprised by the lateness of the hour and how quickly the evening seems to have gone, all ten hours of it.

"What time is your flight tomorrow David?"

"I leave Dorval at 2."

"We plan on leaving soon after breakfast so that we can get Dad back to California by Wednesday and fly home Thursday morning. Why don't we drop you at the airport on our way out of Montreal?"

"Sounds great Mom. Thanks. Well, bed for me." He hugs his mother and warmly shakes hands with everyone and turns to Angelique.

"Thank you for a wonderful evening." Angelique hugs him, liking the young man more every times she sees him. Too bad he and Roni seem to dislike each other. Oh, well.

Mark is last to leave the room. It's obvious that whatever tension might be between him and Jon because of their relationship to Angelique, they admire and respect each other. Mark gives her a quick hug, as if not wanting to upset Jon and the mood of the evening. He walks slowly to his room at the end of the central hallway. Jon and Angelique go upstairs. Ten minutes of ablutions, a good night kiss and they are sound asleep.

Angelique wakes to the smell of coffee. It's after 9 and she's the last downstairs.

"Jon, why didn't you wake me? I feel terrible."

"Strangely enough sweetheart we all know how to make breakfast, so it was a unanimous decision to let you sleep in."

"Well, I thank all of you. I'm starving."

"As you will have noticed, Angelique is always starving and wants to eat the minute her feet hits the floor in the morning."

"I confess. 'tis all true. Let's go into the dining room. This is quite a spread. You've outdone yourself."

They linger over breakfast until David notes the time and they have to get moving. Within fifteen minutes their luggage is stowed in the rental car and it's time for goodbyes. Angelique and Mark are the last to say farewell. He holds Angelique close and presses his lips to her cheek. They linger there and feel so hot it's like she's being branded. He moves away. She lifts her hand, moves her index finger across his chest.

"Fly safely."

His eyes get watery, He lifts her hand to his mouth, kisses her fingers and whispers "I will always love you" into her ear, then slowly gets in to the car. She cannot speak. She waves until the car is out of sight. Jon is aware of the emotion of the moment and says nothing. He puts his arms around her shoulders and suggests they go for a walk. She waits outside while he gets heavy sweaters and they walk for more than an hour enjoying the brisk morning air. By the time they get back to the house Chris, Suzette and the twins are packed and ready to leave.

"We were going to stop at our favourite restaurant in St. Helene for lunch. Why don't you and Mom drive out there? We can all have lunch together then we'll hit the road to Ottawa and you can take a leisurely drive back to Montreal."

"Sounds like a great idea. What do you think Angelique?"

"Excellent. I'll have more time to chat with those grandsons of ours. Give me a few minutes to clean up from breakfast."

"Just get your handbag. Everything is taken care of."

"I'll have to give more dinner parties." Angelique is grateful for the distraction. She doesn't want to have time alone to think. She is confused by the feeling in the pit of her stomach. She wants it to go away. She's also grateful Jon does not ask why she is so emotional.

Over the next few weeks they receive thank you cards from Angeline and Paul and Mark. Angeline says her father is feeling more tired than usual and she's been insisting he see his doctor more often. At Christmas they exchange cards and promises to get together in the summer. They set a tentative date for a visit in late August. Roni would be setting off for university and Angelique and Jon planned to visit Texas with Roni and her parents, fly to Dallas the first week in September to visit Angeline and Paul, then to California to visit Mark.

DALLAS

"It's wonderful to have you here again. Paul and I have been looking forward to it all summer. And I know Dad can't wait to see you again."

"Well, at least Angelique." Laughing, Angeline leaves the table to answer the phone.

"When did it happen? How is he?"

"Oh God. We'll be there as soon as we can get a flight." She hangs up, and bursts into tears.

"It's Dad. He's had another heart attack and he's back in hospital. We have to go. I'm sorry."

"Oh Angeline. We are so sorry. Do you mind if we come with you?"

"Thank you Jon. It would be important to Dad if you did."

They find seats on a flight leaving Dallas at 11:30, quickly pack and head for the airport. There is little conversation. It's 3 a.m. by the time Angeline is unlocking the door to her father's home in Lompoc. They all agree to get some sleep and be at the hospital by 7 a.m.

LOMPOC

As they enter Mark's room in the ICU Angelique is shocked to see him lying so still, connected to a respirator with tubing in both arms and nasal oxygen tubes. She has an urge to lie down beside him and comfort him. His doctor comes into the room.

"He's sedated right now and we'll see how he is doing when that wears off in about an hour. We're not sure yet just how much damage has been done this time. We'll know that once results of the tests we performed last night come back later this morning. If you have any questions, just ask the nurse to call me."

Angeline sits close to her father's bed. She tells him how much she loves him, that she and Paul are there and that Jon and Angelique have also come to see him. Jon and Paul leave to get coffee form the cafeteria.

"I'm so glad you're here Angelique. I'm so afraid I'm going to lose him this time. He's been doing so well I guess I tried to pretend his heart was in better shape because of it."

"We can only hope he has the strength to pull through this one. He's a remarkably strong man. Few would have survived the last attack. He'll feel better just knowing his family is here."

About an hour and a half later the doctor returns, gives Mark an injection and speaks to him.

"Well, you've been giving us another scare. How are you feeling? Can you hear me?"

Mark's eyes flutter. He moves his right hand. Angeline takes it.

"Dad, it's me. Angeline. How are you feeling?" He attempts to squeeze her hand. He opens his eyes.

"Sorry. Hadn't planned on this one. How am I doing doc?"

"Lucky to be alive. You're a damned cat, Forrester. We need you to get lots of rest. We ran some tests and we'll have those back in a couple of hours. I'll let your family stay for now, but they'll have to leave if you get overtired. OK?"

"OK." *As the doctor leaves, Mark turns his head and sees Angelique. His eyes light up and he holds out his hand. She sits beside his bed and takes it.*

"I was expecting to be entertained on this trip. Is this a new way of welcoming your guests?"

"Yeah. Thought it would be an interesting party piece," he says jokingly, in a weak scratchy voice. "Wait 'till you see the encore."

"Just get well again Mark. There's a dance card with your name on it and I plan to collect."

"Jon won't mind?"

"I'm not much for dancing, so I guess I had better not mind. You can do the jiving and I'll do the smooch slow dancing."

"Not quite what I had in mind. But I accept. Angel, how is David?"

"He'd fine. He's flying out to see you tomorrow morning."

Mark tires and they tell him to rest and that they will return later in the afternoon. He is asleep before they get across the room.

"He looks terrible, doesn't he? I'm so afraid we're losing him."

"Let's try to be positive, Angel. We'll know more when we come back and talk to his doctor about those tests. Let's go have lunch and give him a few hours to rest before we come back."

The doctor is with Mark when they return to the hospital. He is off the respirator.

"Well, Mark wants to tell you the results of his tests, so I'm off to do rounds."

"Dad, what did he say?"

"The tests show the damage is not as bad as they thought. But I'm going to be here for a few weeks. The dancing will have to wait for at least another month," he says, looking over at Angelique, then Angeline.

"Now Angel, don't be getting so upset. When I'm not sleeping, I'm looking forward to all the visits you'll be making here. How long will you and Jon be able to stay?"

"We planned to be here until the third week of September, so we're not going anywhere until then. You have plenty of time to get tired of us."

Over the next three days we spend as much time as possible with Mark in his hospital room. Each day there is a noticeable improvement in his condition and spirits. On the fourth day Jon and I decide to have lunch at the Cafe before visiting Mark in the afternoon. We give Hank an update on his friend's state of health and all lift a glass to his continued improvement. He insists we take a bowl of Mark's favourite chowder to the hospital.

Paul is standing outside Mark's room when we return. The look on his face tells us something is wrong.

"He's had another attack. This one is bad."

"He's not…"

"No Angelique. But it's pretty bad. He's been asking for you."

We hurry inside. Angeline is sitting next to Mark's bed holding his hand. Her eyes are red and swollen.

"Dad, Angelique is here."

Mark slowly opens his eyes as Angelique approaches his bedside and takes his hand.

"This is great. We take a couple of hours to have a bite to eat and you do this to yourself. We were just telling Hank you'd probably be showing up for dinner in a week or two. He's counting on it."

Mark smiles. When he speaks his voice is scratchy from the respirator tube he insisted be removed. "Glad you're here. Wish there was more time. Wish so many things. Thank you for coming back to me."

"How could I have resisted a man who went to such lengths to find me."

Mark closes his eyes. He is exhausted but the smile remains. His hold on her hand is a vice grip. She watches Angeline get up to speak to the approaching physician. A lump forms in her throat when she sees him shake his head. Angeline begins to cry. Paul puts his arm around her. They listen quietly to the rest of the news being delivered.

Suddenly, Mark opens his eyes.

"Angeline. Paul." They move closer to the bed. Angeline takes her father's hand.

"Thank you for Angelique. Look after her Paul. You too Angel. I love you very much."

Sobbing, Angeline reaches over to kiss his forehead. "I love you too Dad, too."

"Where's Jon?"

"Here Mark." Jon comes over to the bedside.

"Thank you for sharing Angelique. Look after her."

"Guaranteed Mark. It was great getting to know you."

Mark's breath becomes more labored. He whispers "Angie."

I sit next to him on the bed, holding his icy cold hand.

"I love you."

I lean close to his ear and whisper. He turns to stare at me. His eyes give me a look so filled with love it brings tears. He tries to tug on my hand and I let him lift it. Still staring at me he brings it to his lips and holds it there. Then, as his head falls back on the pillow he drops my hand and closes his eyes. My flyboy has taken one last flight.

His doctor comes into the room to listen to Mark's heart. The slight movement of his head confirms Mark's death. We later learn Mark had talked this moment over with his doctor, aware his heart had reached the end of its life. The next two days are something of a whirlwind. We help Angeline and Paul as much as we can with the various aspects of funeral arrangements. Mark was to be buried in the plot next to Margie.

During the two visitation days before his funeral hundreds of friends, family and fellow military servicemen and officers formed long lines to stop at his coffin to say goodbye. It is strange for Jon and me to be standing in the family line as though we are related in some way. But as Jon points out to me when I express concern, we are, which made me feel somewhat less of an intruder. But there are many moments when it seems like I am in someone else's dream and it makes me feel oddly vulnerable.

The evening before the funeral I answer the doorbell at Angeline and Paul's to find yet another piece of my past in the body of Bridget O'Neill standing on the patio. It had been more than forty years and I still recognize her.

"Angeline called me. I'm so sorry. I had to come."

"Bridget I can't believe I am actually seeing you again." We hug and suddenly we're teenagers again. I invite her in and after an hour of pleasantries with the family we talk until late into the night, catching up on a lifetime apart, all cemented by a short but unforgettable, shared experience.

On the day of the funeral family members are given a final moment with Mark before he is lost to us forever. Looking at him in his flying officers' dress uniform with his wings pinned proudly on his chest, I see him at twenty-seven. Stepping closer, I run my finger across his wings.

"Fly safely, Flyboy."

In that moment I felt as bereft as he must have felt that long ago September as I walked away from him. The loss is so terribly painful it makes me wince. Suddenly weak, I feel a supporting hand beneath my elbow. It's Jon, always looking after me.

"Are you OK sweetheart?"

"Yes. Just very sad." He holds me. "I know. And I understand." As it has always been, there is no need for more. We take our seats and turn to the see Roni being escorted to a chair next to me. I look at her, shocked.

"I had to come G'mere. I'm so sorry about your flyboy," she says kindly. "He was a great guy."

She leans over to hug me, then her grandfather, who is just as surprised to see her but says nothing. It's Roni after all and nothing that child does would ever surprise him.

The funeral service is as uplifting as Mark would have wanted. It is evident he had touched many lives and had many friends who loved him dearly. Some of the eulogies are profound, some emotional and many quite hilarious. The most touching comes from Angeline. I must admit I was concerned she might mention me, but to my relief she makes only an oblique, amusing reference to her father's love for her mother, his daughter and a special woman who once wore a dark, pink hat.

The more than three hundred attending Mark's funeral also came to the reception at the Cafe, where Hank is inconsolable. If anyone else wonders who I really am or why I appear so intimately involved with the family they don't ask and no one volunteers information beyond the "family friend" nature of the relationship.

Everything moves in slow motion and it is strange to think I wouldn't see Mark again, even though I remind myself this was inevitable, given that it was the serious condition of his heart that brought us together again. Bridget flew back to Boston the next morning and all too soon Jon and I are in our room getting ready to catch a noon flight from Lompoc.

Roni was flying back to Austin later in the afternoon and David planned to stay in Lompoc until the end of the week. We all have breakfast together, all feeling a profound sense of loss. Jon went to collect our luggage from the bedroom and Angeline asks me to come into the living room with her. Once there she opens a hat box and removes the object that had brought us all together.

"Dad asked me to make sure I give this to you before you left. It's only right you should have it and it does belong to you."

"Are you sure Angeline? I would be happy to leave it here with you."

"No. Please. Dad made it clear you are to have it and I want to honour that wish."

"Thank you Angeline. Thank you for coming to find me. I am so happy to have been able to see Mark again. This may have been a very strange and unusual situation but seeing him was very special to me. So thank you. And Paul."

Angeline returns the hat to the box and replaces the lid. Jon appears with the luggage and they set off for the airport.

"Don't forget me G'mere. I'll be home for Christmas. Love you. By G'pere. Love you too."

When I turn to say goodbye to Angeline she is crying.

"I'm sorry. I know it sounds crazy but I feel as though I'm losing another member of the family."

"But I'll be back and I hope you'll come to see us again in Montreal."

"Thank you. I was hoping you would ask." We all laugh. Mark would be pleased.

The flight home is uneventful. Jon immerses himself in an old western on the small TV in front of him and I prefer to day dream. I think of the pink hat ensconced in its box in the overhead and the way it came to control so many lives. I say a silent prayer for the wonderful man I married and a silent thank you to him for not asking what I had said to the wonderful man I didn't.

Some things are best left unsaid.

LOMPOC. *Eight Years Later*

"Tell me again why we had to come here to the cemetery before I leave for overseas," the Air Force Captain says to his new bride.

"I wanted to say thank you to your grandfather for bringing us together. If he had not loved my grandmother we would have never met.

"That's an excellent reason. I'm sure he would approve."

The young man holds out his hand. "I love you Roni." She takes his hand. "I love you David."

"Let's go. You look gorgeous in that pink hat. He would definitely approve."

"Me and my Flyboy."

They walk away, laughing. Together.

EPILOGUE

Two months after her father's funeral Angeline began the sad reality of getting her parents' home ready for its new owners.

In the process of cleaning out her father's desk she finds a large, locked, yellow box with a small brass key taped to the bottom. It is evident from the discoloration of the tape that the box had never been opened. Her mother's name is printed on a small oval tag in the upper right hand corner.

A wave of loss assails her as she runs her fingers softly over the lid. Her hands shake as she pulls off the key and inserts it into the lock. She hears a clicking sound, pulls out the key and slowly lifts the lid. Inside are personal papers belonging to her mother including old letters from friends, postcards, birthday and Christmas cards, cards with childish printing that read "I love you Mom, from Angeline." As she reads each one she stacks them in a pile on the desk. The last envelope has Angeline written in her mother's calligraphy-style handwriting. Seeing it brings tears.

Reaching in again she picks it up, opens it and pulls out two sheets of folded paper. Unfolding them she reads:

> *My dearest Angeline,*
>
> *When you read this I will no longer be with you. It may be that your father will have joined me in my sleep. I am certain that by now you probably know the story about your father and Angelique. Do not judge him harshly for loving two women in his lifetime. You see I knew in my heart, in some strange way I can't explain, that his deep love for her allowed him to love me so dearly.*
>
> *I want to tell you about the amazing night when we were just friends and he became quite drunk. Earlier in the day we had gone to the beach and had so much fun. I could tell that he was a cut above most of the young pilots I met. Later,*

he took me to one of his favourite restaurants for dinner and afterwards we went to the Tikki bar on the beach for a nightcap. I sipped white wine while he drank many beers. At around 2 a.m. he began telling me about Angelique, how he wanted to marry her and she refused. He told me the only thing he had left of her was a big brimmed, dark pint hat.

You deserve to understand why I never told your father I knew about Angelique and her hat and why I wanted to be the woman who would be his only other love.

At the bottom of this box is a dairy I kept at the time. Open it at the page where you'll find a pink ribbon.

I love you dear Angeline.
Remember me.

Read more about the continuing saga of

the characters you have met in future books

about their adventures and misadventures.

THOUGHTS